MISS PRIM AND
THE MAVERICK
MILLIONAIRE

MISS PRIM AND THE MAVERICK MILLIONAIRE

BY

NINA SINGH

MILLS & BOON™

First published in Great Britain 2017
By Mills & Boon, an imprint of HarperCollins*Publishers*
1 London Bridge Street, London, SE1 9GF

Large Print edition 2017

© 2017 Nilay Nina Singh

ISBN: 978-0-263-07130-6

Printed and bound in Great Britain
by CPI Antony Rowe, Chippenham, Wiltshire

For my wonderful husband and children.
Thank you for all the patience,
faith and support. Not to mention
the many very needed nudges.

And for the best group of fellow
writer friends I could have ever hoped for.

CHAPTER ONE

THIS DEFINITELY WASN'T in her job description.

Jenna Townsend glanced at her watch, not actually noting the time. Then glanced at it again. A car should be picking him up from the airport right at this moment. Which meant he would be here at her office within the hour. She took a too-large swig of coffee and gasped as it burned her tongue and throat. Why was she so nervous? Babysitting the CEO of Jordan's Fine Jewelry for the next several days shouldn't warrant this much anxiety.

Cabe Jordan, CEO extraordinaire, was on his way back to Boston. The man who'd taken the small business his parents started in the historic North End and made it one of the most profitable national corporations of the last decade.

Hard to believe they'd grown up together in the

same small town just outside Boston. Two years ahead of her in school, Cabe had been her older brother's bane of existence, besting Sam at everything. Her brother had not been happy when she'd taken the position of regional manager and started working for his nemesis. But opportunities like this weren't ones to be passed up, not for someone like her.

The job had been everything she could have hoped for and more. Until the email in her inbox the other day "requesting" her assistance in escorting Mr. Jordan as he revisited the flagship Boston site. For some reason, he'd specifically requested that she be his local liaison on this trip. Jenna shook her head.

Why did he need one anyway?

She'd felt like she'd been sent to the principal's office, unable to shake the feeling that he was really here to check up on *her*. Had she done something wrong? Let something crucial slip through the cracks? Or had he woken up one day and realized he'd hired a small-town hick with no real-world experience. Maybe he was looking to replace her with some hotshot MBA from a real business school and he wanted to tell her in person. Maybe Sam had been right all these years and Cabe Jordan really was an elitist who had always looked down his nose at people like her.

Heavens, she had to get a grip. And try to stay positive. There could very well be a good reason for Cabe's visit. Hadn't she just come across an internal email regarding an opening in upper-level management? Perhaps he was here to tell her she was being promoted. It was possible. After all, her numbers spoke for themselves.

Did she dare to hope? Her job here meant so much for both her future and everyone who depended on her.

A quick knock on the door preceded the abrupt entrance of her assistant carrying a gleaming silver tray laden with pastries, a coffeepot and two brand-new porcelain mugs. Nothing but the best for Mr. Jordan.

"Thanks, Nora," Jenna said as she set the tray down on a side bureau.

"You got it. Do we know his ETA yet?"

"Won't be much longer now."

Nora put her hand over her heart, a dreamy, far-away expression on her face. "I wonder if he'll have Carmen with him."

"Carmen?"

"You know, that Spanish model he was photographed with recently."

Jenna shrugged. "I wouldn't know."

"Oh, come on. You have to be as curious as the rest of us. He's been spotted out and about with at least three different beauties in the last month alone."

Jenna merely smiled. If she was curious about anything, it was the reason for this whole trip to begin with. "Mr. Jordan's personal affairs are none of my concern. I simply work for the man."

"And what a dreamy man he is." Despite being a happily married grandmother of a newly born infant, Nora was unabashed in her appreciation of handsome men.

"Be that as it may…" Jenna brushed an imaginary piece of lint off her right shoulder. This conversation was making her uncomfortable.

Cabe had always been an endless source of gossip around here. She understood the curiosity—of course she did. Handsome, successful, mysterious. Cabe had really made a name for himself in the retail jewelry business. But endless speculation about the man wouldn't get her a regular paycheck.

"I should probably get back to work on this presentation I set up for him." She glanced at the graphic on her screen. She'd worked all night on it, taking the initiative to put together a slide presentation for Cabe's review. Even though she didn't know the exact reason for his visit, she figured presenting him with some specifics on the current business numbers wouldn't hurt.

"I'm sure you'll impress him, dear. Please don't fret."

Nora, of all people, knew how much Jenna needed this job. Her school loans alone were enough to keep her in debt for a good portion of her adult life. But as far as assurances went, Jenna wasn't convinced.

"It can't hurt to be prepared."

"Of course, dear." Taking the hint, Nora walked out of the office, gently shutting the door behind her. As much as she wanted to relax about all this, Jenna couldn't seem to heed Nora's advice not to "fret."

She had to face it. Whatever his reasons, for the next several days, she would have to be Cabe Jordan's glorified and overqualified chaperone. If only she could figure out why he needed one.

The only thing draped on Cabe's arm when he walked in was his suit jacket. Not that she'd really thought he'd have a date with him when he came into the office. Though if the gossip websites were to be believed, he didn't travel far without female companionship. Jenna stood as she eyed him in the reception area, chatting with Nora.

She watched as he walked over to the doorway of her office. Dressed in a well-tailored suit that fit him like a glove, he looked impeccable. Tall, still fit. Jenna drew in a deep breath. Those websites hadn't done him justice. She'd refused to acknowledge it since receiving that email, but the truth was absolutely impossible to ignore now. The silly schoolgirl crush she'd had on him as a kid hadn't abated one iota.

Well, if he was out of reach then, he was downright unattainable now. Still, like Nora, she could certainly appreciate his...pure masculinity.

Snap out of it.

He was waiting for her to invite him in as she stood there with her mouth gaping open. Staring at him. How utterly unprofessional. So much for coming across as the dynamic, invaluable employee Cabe's company couldn't do without.

"Mr. Jordan. So nice to see you here. Come in. Please."

Wow, now she was positively dazzling him with her talent for witty conversation. He strode into the room and gave her a warm smile that sent electric volts down to her toes.

"Jenna. We've known each other a long time. Please call me Cabe."

He spoke the words cordially enough, but she couldn't shake the feeling that she sensed some subtle undertone, some kind of underlying message. Or maybe that was just her silly attraction to him that she'd thought she had gotten over eons ago. She'd been so wrong about that.

Definitely not the time to realize it.

She gave her head a brisk shake to clear it. She could not blow this initial meeting. She had the distinct impression the future of her livelihood depended on it.

"Would you like a cup of coffee? Cabe."

His smile grew wider. "That's more like it. And I'd love some coffee. But only if you'll join me."

She nodded and moved to the serving tray. Cabe held up a hand to stop her. "Please, let me."

Really? *He* was going to serve *her*?

"How do you take it?"

"Just cream, please."

He poured with a steady hand, doctored it with the small pitcher of creamer and handed her the cup. He poured a cup straight black for himself before sitting down across from her desk. In the smaller chair.

Was it her or was Cabe going out of his way

to make her feel less of his employee and more of his equal?

Jenna cleared her throat. "So, what brings you here?"

He shrugged. "Just figured it's about time I visit the flagship Boston site. Now that the Manhattan store is thriving, I can devote some attention to other areas. This is where it all began, after all. Feel I may have been neglecting it over the years."

Did he mean it would have fared better if he'd been more involved? But the regional New England stores were doing fine with her at the helm. Sales had grown progressively over the years. Not at an astronomical pace but pretty steady, despite the slow economy. Heavens, why such paranoia?

"I see."

"Just for a few days."

"Well, I think you'll be pleased with the overall numbers. Here, let me show you." She walked over to the other side of the desk to face her laptop and motioned for him to follow.

Mistake. She hadn't thought to pull over another chair facing the computer. They had no choice but to stand side by side. He smelled of pine and sandalwood.

She pushed herself to go through each slide, hardly aware of content. She stammered on every other sentence. Hopefully, she was at least coherent.

Cabe nodded at all the right points, so that was at least encouraging. He also asked some pertinent questions that Jenna was blessedly prepared for. Still, when she finished with her presentation, she felt as if she'd just trekked the full length of the Freedom Trail. And felt just as out of breath.

If Cabe noticed, he was too much of a gentleman to let on. "Very impressive," he said, still staring at the upward slope of the graph on the last slide.

"Thank you."

"Both the performance numbers and your presentation."

"Thank you." Again with the witty conversation.

"I'm not surprised. You're a very capable regional manager."

Don't you dare say "thank you" again. She simply nodded, tried not to duck her head at the praise. The burning in her cheeks crept clear up to her scalp. She resisted the urge to fan herself like an old-fashioned Southern belle.

He did seem genuinely impressed. Maybe she'd been wrong to be so nervous. Perhaps he really was here to talk to her about a promotion. Stranger things had happened.

She decided to take a chance. "Oh. Well, then. Excuse me, Mr. Jordan—"

He interrupted her. "Cabe."

She smiled politely. "I mean Cabe. If you don't mind my asking… Why are you really here? After all this time. What aren't you telling me?"

Cabe's response died on his lips as the older secretary entered Jenna's office. "Excuse me, Mr. Jordan. There's a call on the office phone for you, from Corporate."

He fished his cell out of his pocket, realizing he'd left it in airplane mode after his flight. "Thanks, Nora." Sure enough, the phone started buzzing as soon as he changed the setting. A naughty text from Carmen popped up. He tried not to groan out loud. The woman could be draining. He would have to do something about that pretty soon. She had her sights on something that wasn't going to happen. He'd have to find a way to let her down gently. No doubt it would cost him a pretty penny.

Then there were numerous messages from his assistant in New York, no doubt about the Caribbean expansion deal. Nothing about the project so far had run smoothly.

And so it began.

The interruption was just as well. He wasn't sure how much he could share with Jenna Townsend just yet. Sharp as she was, she'd surmised that something else had prompted his visit.

He wanted to believe there'd been some kind of mistake, that she had no involvement. But it wouldn't be the first time he'd misjudged someone.

"Would you mind if I take this, Jenna?"

She shook her head. "Of course not." She walked toward the door. "I'll give you some privacy."

"There's no need for that." But she'd already left by the time he reached for her desk phone.

Cabe hung up the phone several minutes later and tried not to curse in frustration. He'd been right. There were indeed yet more complications on the resort island where he planned to open a new high-end retail jewelry store, this time to do with zoning issues.

He would have to fly down there. The sooner the better. Which meant he had to wrap up here in Boston as quickly as he could. He had to address the real purpose of this visit. Of all the reasons to have to come back, a thieving employee. He shook his head at the utter surprise of it. There was absolutely no reason for an employee to steal from him. The company paid well and provided numerous benefits. The only reason had to be greed.

His head of security assured Cabe that such thefts were usually inside jobs, almost always involving the store manager, who in this case was Jenna Townsend. The timing couldn't have been worse—Jenna had been on track for a major promotion before the theft came to light.

As soon as he'd heard the name, he'd wanted to deal with the matter himself. He'd hired Jenna personally. His parents had always been quite fond of her. They'd asked him to give Jenna a chance when she'd graduated top of her class from business school two years ago. Despite what the town had thought about the Townsend family and its troubled history over the years, his parents had insisted that Jenna was cut from a different cloth and that she just needed a chance to prove it. His mom and dad were all about giving people a chance. He liked to think that had served them well, at least as far as their son was concerned.

Cabe's original plan was to spend a few days with her. Maybe even find some evidence. So he'd asked for her specifically to be his assistant on this trip. But now he had forty-eight hours at the most before he had to fly to the Caribbean to deal with the other pressing matter. That left him with only one choice. He had to come right out and ask her what, if anything, she knew about the missing jewelry.

He could be quite persuasive when he had to be. Besides, he didn't have the time to dwell on this. He had to get to the bottom of it all and move on to business as usual.

No one stole from Cabe Jordan and got away with it.

When Jenna returned to her office, Nora ran fast on her heels. "Is there anything else I can do for you, Mr. Jordan?" the older woman asked as she cleared the tray of mugs and coffee pitcher.

Cabe turned and flashed them both a smile that made Jenna's knees go weak. "As a matter of fact, you can, Nora," he replied. "Please clear Jenna's calendar for the next two hours or so and cancel her appointments."

What? Why?

To her shock and horror, he added, "I'd like to take my regional manager to lunch."

Oh, no. She had to nip this in the bud right now.

She did not want to sit across a table from this man, just the two of them. She was absolutely no good at small talk. And her presentation earlier had covered all the business details she could possibly bring up. Whatever he had to tell her, he could do so right here in this office. "I'm afraid I just can't do that, Mr. Jord—"

"Cabe."

She took a steadying breath. "I can't steal away for lunch today, Cabe." She glanced at Nora, willing her to help. Instead, Nora threw her overboard.

"Nonsense. Of course she can. There's nothing pressing on her calendar this afternoon. And she hardly ever eats a real lunch. Usually a granola bar at her desk as she continues to work."

Cabe's smile dripped with satisfaction. "It's settled, then. Do you have a preference where to eat, Jenna?"

She could only shake her head.

He led her gently to the door. "How about Nawlin's, that sidewalk café on Newbury, then? It's a pleasant enough day to eat outside and I've missed their sandwiches."

Like it mattered. As if she'd be able to taste anything. She'd be lucky if she could keep it down.

"That's fine." Only it wasn't fine at all, and her stomach did another little flip to prove it.

The queasiness hadn't subsided at all ten minutes later when Cabe pulled a chair out for her at the quaint outdoor café on one of Boston's swankiest streets. The lunch crowd milled and bustled around them. Two food trucks parked nearby had lines several feet long. All in all, a perfect day to enjoy a leisurely meal outside. If only she could enjoy it.

Their food came out in no time. She was picking at her Caesar salad when things went from bad to catastrophic. Cabe was going to try to make small talk. And his first choice of topic: the absolute last thing in the world she wanted to get into right now.

"So, Jenna. If I recall, you have an older brother."

She had to discuss her broken, dysfunctional family, with none other than Cabe Jordan.

"Yes. Sam. You two must have been in a few of the same classes."

"It was just the two of you and your mom, right? How is she, by the way? Do I recall she hadn't been feeling well for a while?"

Jenna's blood froze in her veins and she lost her grip on her fork. It fell to her plate with a clatter so loud the sound echoed through the air. Of course he must have heard rumblings over the years. Stories about Amanda tended to get around.

Cabe stopped eating and stared at her.

She stammered for a response. There was no good way to talk about her mother. "Yes. Yes, she's doing better." Such a lie.

Cabe stopped eating. "I'm so sorry, Jenna. I hope it isn't anything too serious."

She so didn't want to go down this path. Any topic but her mother. Anything but discussing Amanda and her problems in front of this perfect man who grew up with the perfect family in his perfect home. But what choice did she have? He waited for an answer, staring at her expectantly.

"Uh…she actually is ill. In a way." She took a deep breath. "My mother's been having a hard time the past few years. Trying to kick a drug and alcohol problem."

Cabe blinked at her. Clearly, he hadn't seen that coming.

"She's trying really hard," Jenna added. Another lie.

In fact, her mother had just shown up at her door last night, asking for money for "groceries." When Jenna had insisted on taking her to the market herself, Amanda had grown violent, shattering a vase on her hardwood floor before storming out. She'd wanted groceries of the more liquid variety. It had been the last thing Jenna had needed as she'd been trying to finish up her presentation for today. Thanks to Amanda's visit, she'd been up most of the night due to the upsetting interruption.

"I'm sorry to hear that," Cabe said in a gentle and soothing voice.

"I'm sure you're a tremendous source of support for your mother," he continued. "She's lucky to have you."

Though her mother didn't see it that way. In Amanda's eyes, Jenna always came up short. Even though if Jenna hadn't stepped in on numerous occasions, Amanda would no doubt be in jail. Or worse.

"I'm doing what I can to help her."

Cabe cleared his throat. The look he gave her was so understanding, so gentle that it made her breath catch. "It's quite admirable that you're trying to help your mother."

Oh, heavens. What could she say to that? She didn't have a choice but to help her mother. Otherwise, she and her brother would be left to deal with the cleanup.

"Thanks."

Several moments passed in awkward silence. So awkward that she wanted to give the waitress a hug when she interrupted to fill their glasses.

Jenna watched her leave before hesitantly turning her gaze back to Cabe. He gave her an unreadable look. Curiosity? Admiration?

She didn't and couldn't care. What did it matter what Cabe Jordan thought of her or her broken family? In a few days, he'd be gone from Boston and hopefully he wouldn't return for another three to four years. He would just go back to being nothing more than an electronic signature at the bottom of her office emails.

But for now, she still had to get through this godforsaken lunch with him sitting right across from her.

He'd never understand, Jenna thought as she pretended to eat. Even under the best of circumstances, she'd never be in league with people like Cabe or even his parents, who had always been so sweet to her. Cabe had probably never had to hide from a drunken tirade or had to clean up after a parent who'd barreled in at three in the morning then promptly gotten sick all over the carpet.

She and Cabe Jordan may have grown up in the same town, but they were from two different worlds.

CHAPTER TWO

CABE PUSHED HIS plate away with half his sandwich still untouched. He'd lost his appetite. Clearly, Jenna had none, either, since she did nothing more than move lettuce around her plate.

He couldn't help but wonder. Maybe Jenna indeed did have some involvement in the jewelry theft. Was her mother in that much trouble that Jenna may have needed a large supply of cash to help her? Cabe didn't want to believe the worst, but his manager of security had been adamant that Jenna may indeed know something.

Damn. That would change things. Though wrong and criminal, if Jenna was guilty, she hadn't done it for herself but for her mother. She'd practically just admitted that she would do whatever she could to help her parent.

He'd decided back at the office that he wouldn't

ask her about it there. Not in front of her friends and colleagues. So he'd taken her to lunch instead.

Now he just wanted to know the truth. He wanted to tell her he could help. That in turn she could get her mother some help.

After all, he and Jenna Townsend were not that different under the surface. His life could have easily turned out as difficult as hers if not for the random hand of fate all those years ago. Pure luck so often determined the entirety of one's life. He knew how lucky he'd been.

"Listen, Jenna," he began, not sure exactly where to start. Business school didn't prepare you for every scenario. "About my visit to Boston. There's something I came here specifically to see you about."

"Yes?" Her question was barely a whisper.

"I want you to know that I can be a friend as well as your corporate CEO."

Was she trembling? "You can be straight with me," he added. "I hope you realize that."

She gave her head a quick shake. "I'm afraid I don't understand."

"You really don't have anything you might want to talk about? Regarding the store, perhaps?"

"No. Not really." She swallowed. "Have I done something wrong?"

Cabe leaned back in his chair. If she did know anything, then she had the acting skills of a Hollywood-caliber actress. "Huh. You really have no idea what I might be talking about?"

"Not a clue."

Cabe tried to regroup. Damn. This conversation was becoming way too messy. "Allow me to explain. A routine inventory check last week by security resulted in a troubling discovery."

She sucked her bottom lip, and heaven help him, he lost his focus for a split second. "Why wasn't I made aware of this? As the regional manager of that store?"

"It's our policy to keep such matters quiet until a thorough investigation."

She gave her head a quick shake. "Investigation? What exactly was this troubling discovery?"

"One of the more valuable pieces seems to be missing. A bracelet."

Cabe watched as understanding dawned. Jenna sucked in a breath and grew as pale as the white linen tablecloth. "Oh, my God. You think I took it."

Whoa. He hadn't expected her to go there quite so soon. "Jenna, wait just a second—"

Her cheeks suddenly grew cherry red. "That's why you came down here yourself. You think I stole from my own store. You think I stole from *you*!"

It came so fast he didn't have time to react. Before he knew it, he wore the rest of his sandwich on his lap and his shirt was drenched in iced tea.

As he watched her storm away, Cabe came to three distinct conclusions. One, Jenna Townsend moved as fast as a prizefighter ducking a punch. Second, judging by her confusion and the vehemence of her reaction, she was most definitely innocent.

And third, if he didn't get to the bottom of it all real soon, he was likely to lose a damn talented regional manager.

Stupid. Stupid. Stupid. She would never learn.

Jenna bypassed the elevator and ran up the three flights of stairs to get to the floor that housed her office. She didn't want to risk running into anyone. How would she explain the tears?

To think, for a while there she'd believed Cabe Jordan might actually be in town to promote her! What a laugh. Instead, he'd accused her of stealing from him.

People like her weren't promoted to corporate-level positions. They were suspected of thievery. They were the first ones investigated when valuable jewelry went missing.

People like her dumped food on others' laps.

She tried to take a deep breath. She probably shouldn't have done that. It was reckless and impulsive. Rather than calmly and reasonably defending herself, she'd let her emotions take over. She'd succumbed to the urge to lash out.

Just as her mother would have done.

And she was her mother's daughter. The apple and the tree and all that. Why did she ever think she could escape that simple truth? The rest of the world wouldn't ever let her forget that fact.

It didn't matter how hard she worked, or how many hours she put in. All the years of studying and working her butt off didn't mean a thing to people like Cabe Jordan. The only thing they saw when they looked at her was where she'd come from.

She'd been fooling herself.

Well, if Cabe hadn't intended to fire her right there on the spot, there was no doubt he would now. She'd dumped his lunch in his lap! Never mind that she'd never actually stolen anything. She wouldn't even get a chance to defend her innocence now.

She no doubt should have handled it better. But she'd been barely functioning given what little sleep she'd gotten and the stress of being prepared for Cabe's visit.

How could he have even suggested such a thing?

She didn't realize she'd asked the question out loud until a voice across the room responded.

"Trust me, it wasn't easy."

Jenna's head snapped up. Cabe stood in her office doorway, pants stained and shirt wet. She resisted the urge to cover her mouth in horror.

She pulled her planner out of the desk drawer. "I was just leaving."

"Could you recommend a good dry cleaner first?"

He had the nerve to joke at her predicament? God help her, if the coffee tray were still here she might have very well dumped more on him.

"Jenna, listen—"

"What?" she interrupted. "What could you possibly say to me? Do you want me to confess?"

He stepped into the room and shut the door gently behind him. "I simply want to talk."

"About how I stole from you?"

"I was given the information from my head of security. About a theft at the Boston store."

She crossed her arms in front of her chest. "Right. And then you decided that if something had been stolen, it must have been that no-good Jenna Townsend. She must have had a hand in the whole mess. It only makes sense. She comes from bad stock. She's never had much to begin with and she can't be trusted."

"Jenna, stop. That's not how this all came to be."

She merely glared at him. How dare he deny it?

He walked up to where she stood and gestured to the chair. "Please sit."

"Why? Would you like to accuse me some more? Should I call an attorney?" Now that she'd said it, she had the frightening thought that she may actually need one.

Her vision grew dark. This couldn't be happening. After today she may very well have no job. And no hope of finding one if word got out that she couldn't be trusted. Despite all the years of hard work and sacrifice, she was going to end up penniless on the street. Exactly what she'd feared all along.

To think, the cause of her nightmare would be none other than Cabe Jordan, the man of her teenage daydreams. Who would have thought?

"Jenna, let's try to talk this out."

She lifted her bag. "Perhaps you want to go through this. Maybe pat me down before you let me go."

He blinked. "Pat you down? No. Of course not. I just want to clear all this up." He leaned over with both palms on the desk between them. "About a week ago my head of security requested an urgent meeting. Apparently, someone realized that a piece of rare jewelry at the Boston store had been switched out during a routine security department inventory. The real piece had been replaced with a cheap replica that looked exactly like the original."

"And you assumed I did it. Because you know where I come from and what I might be capable of."

He held one hand up. "Hold on. That's not what happened. The management team is always considered under such circumstances. It's just routine."

At her silence, he continued. "Additionally, there's an electronic log of anyone who's used their key to access that particular case, the one with the higher-end items. Your key was the one used."

Her blood went cold. But that just couldn't be. "Who says?"

"My head of security up at headquarters. He's always been very good at his job. I had no reason to distrust him."

Of course he didn't. "But you had every reason to distrust me."

Something shifted in his eyes. "Listen, Jenna. The only reason I came here personally was because it was you. I wanted to get to the bottom of it myself, do some investigating. But there's a sudden matter that needs my attention with a store opening in the Caribbean. I have to get down there. In my haste, I handled it very badly. I see that now."

People tended to do that with her, rush to judgment. She couldn't expect to be granted the benefit of the doubt, not given where she came from. Cabe may claim objectivity by saying he came to look into the matter personally, but it hardly mattered. No, she would have to find a way to fully clear her name, in such a way that there would never be any more doubt.

"There has to be some kind of mistake," she muttered, trying to think. There had to be an explanation, a way to prove her innocence. But how? She suddenly felt deflated. How could this be happening? Pulling out her desk chair, she plopped herself into it.

A sudden, encouraging thought occurred to her. She looked up at him. "The video? There has to be video footage. We have cameras all over the store."

He gave her a sympathetic look. "The video surveillance system was conveniently disengaged for a forty-eight-hour period on the fifteenth and sixteenth of last month. We believe that's when the theft occurred."

Oh, God. His words knocked the wind right out of her. If there was no video to exonerate her, she had no other ideas. Her eyes began to sting.

There was nothing she could do, no way to clear her name. She had no job. She had no real family. She'd probably end up with a criminal record. Despite everything, all the years of busting her behind to get ahead, she'd end up like her mom after all.

Cabe Jordan would always question whether she was a no-good thief.

Wait a minute.

She snapped her head up. "Wait. What date did you just say? The fifteenth of March?"

He nodded. "Yes, that's correct."

"You're certain?"

"That's what I was told."

She knew it! Hopeful relief surged in her chest. "Cabe, I wasn't even in town the week of the fifteenth. I was away at a jewelry designers' expo in San Diego."

He quirked an eyebrow. "And?"

"And my keys were safely locked up in the main vault right here in this building. Including the one that would have opened that particular case. I have proof."

* * *

He didn't want to examine why he was so relieved. For some reason, Cabe had been hopeful
all along that Jenna was completely innocent.
And apparently she could prove it. "Proof? You
have a way to prove your key was locked up?"

She nodded triumphantly. "Yes. The security
officer on call the day before I left signed off on
the paperwork. All my keys were locked up in
the main vault before I left. Safe and secure."

"That's the correct protocol. Where is this security officer now?"

She shrugged. "I don't know. I'm not the one
in charge of hiring and managing security."

Cabe pinched the bridge of his nose. "I have a
sneaking suspicion he's no longer working for us.
And that he has a very valuable piece of jewelry
in his possession."

Jenna stood staring at him with satisfaction,
clearly enjoying the upper hand. So she was indeed innocent. Just as he'd hoped. Heaven help
him, he had to resist the urge to go and hug her.
Not that she would have it.

"Guess your security head isn't as thorough as you would like to think," she said.

"In his defense, he's going through a rough patch personally. Clearly, it's affected his professional duties. I'll have a word with him."

She rolled her eyes at him and muttered something under her breath. He thought he heard the words "That's rich."

"Jenna, I know an apology isn't nearly enough. But it's all I have. My only excuse is that I've been swamped with various small projects as well as a major international expansion. I rushed and acted on something that I should have taken the time to examine more closely. I'm deeply, resolutely sorry."

Her face softened, and the effect nearly knocked him off his feet. "Thank you for that," she said simply, genuinely. "And I'm sorry for... you know." She pointed to his drenched clothing.

"Nah, don't mention it. I daresay I deserved a good food toss." He was also admittedly relieved. He didn't have to fire a dedicated and competent employee after all. That left only one problem.

Things were extremely awkward now with a star employee who deserved better treatment than he'd just doled out. He had a major mea culpa on his hands. As usual, he had rushed to judgment, merely to save some time. Once again, he'd acted without fully thinking through the issue. Not a good attribute in a CEO, yet another character trait he had to work on.

First thing first. Somehow, someway, he had to make this all up to Jenna.

He was getting ready to say so when her assistant knocked and entered her office.

Nora stopped in her tracks when she saw the state of Cabe's clothing. "I'm sorry," she began. "Am I interrupting?"

"That's okay, Nora. What is it?" Jenna behaved like the consummate professional, addressing her admin as if nothing was wrong.

"The Wellesley store just called. They're panicked about their staffing shortage," Nora told her, her gaze still leveled at Cabe.

"I made two very strong offers this morning,"

Jenna said. "I have no doubt both candidates will take the job. Is that all?"

"One more thing," Nora continued. "The store manager at the Burlington site called again complaining about the lack of shelf space."

Jenna nodded. "Real Estate just called this morning about the sewing shop next door. It's finally shutting down, so we can take the space over. We'll sign the lease within the week."

Cabe watched in admiration. *Damn.* She really was good. Given her background and her hardships growing up, she couldn't have gotten this far in life without being smart and disciplined. Would he have fared as well? He had to wonder. If fate hadn't stepped in and turned his life in a different direction, would he have figured out a way to pull himself up the way Jenna Townsend had? All on his own, like her? Or would he have ended up on the streets? Or locked up in a cell somewhere? Or worse.

Jordan's Fine Jewelry absolutely could not lose someone like Jenna. Not for any reason, the least of which being his stupidity. If only he had someone like her in charge of the Caribbean project.

There it was.

The idea made perfect sense. Before this whole theft fiasco, Jenna's name had come up several times whenever a high-level position opened up at Corporate. She was already due for a promotion.

Perhaps he had a way to salvage the mess he'd made of this whole visit. And possibly even help himself in the process. He was about to make a very strong offer, too. One he hoped Jenna could not refuse. First, he had to get her to listen to him. And forget about what he'd almost just accused her of.

As soon as Nora left, Jenna stood and glared at him. "Well, now what, Mr. Jordan. Am I still under investigation?"

He reached out to gently take her by the arm. "Absolutely not. On the contrary, I need to show you how sorry I am."

She looked down at his hand, then back with clearly puzzled eyes. "Show me?"

"I assumed my security head knew what he was doing, Jenna. Please understand."

She stood silent, clearly not ready to cut him any slack. And why should she? He deserved her derision. How could he have let this happen? He hated looking misinformed. Or worse, appearing incompetent. Mistakes were a luxury he wouldn't allow himself in his position.

"You're one of the best regional managers we have at Jordan's Fine Jewelry," he continued. "I should have handled this differently. And I don't want to lose you over some…misunderstanding."

She visibly bristled. He really wasn't very good at saying sorry, not having had much experience. She had no idea how hard he was trying.

"This was more than a mere misunderstanding."

He nodded. "I realize that. I think I can make it up to you."

She pulled her arm free. But she was clearly listening. "How?"

"I could use the services of a competent and

experienced regional manager to help me with a project."

Her chin lifted. "What kind of project?"

"I'm sure you know we're trying to expand internationally, starting with the opening of a new store in the Caribbean."

"Yes, I know."

"You should also know that so far it hasn't gone at all smoothly. In fact, I need to be there within two days to put out the latest fire."

She narrowed her gaze on him. "What does that have to do with me?"

"Come with me, Jenna."

It took a moment to process Cabe's words. "Are you offering me another job?"

He nodded. "One that comes with a higher title. And the adequate adjustment in pay, obviously."

Jenna's head spun. Within the span of a few minutes, she'd gone from decrying the loss of her next paycheck to being offered a promotion. If she examined the matter too closely, Cabe's offer might very well be construed as a bribe.

But it was also an opportunity of a lifetime. A very tempting one.

Cabe motioned to her desk chair. "Please have a seat. Let's discuss this."

Her pride pushed her to turn her back and walk away, slam the door on her way out. Her business-school-trained brain had other ideas.

Begrudgingly, she pulled out her chair and sat down. "What exactly did you have in mind?"

The look of relief on his face sent an odd shiver down her spine. She didn't dare read too much into it.

"I'm tired of trying to get this new site up and running by myself. I've been meaning to hire someone. You're perfect for the job."

"Cabe, you can't just expect me to forget that you were ready to believe I may be capable of theft."

"But that's exactly what I'm asking you to do," he said with the confidence of a successful tycoon who's used to getting his own way. "Rather than spend inordinate time on an extensive talent search, I'd like to offer you the position. You've been considered for several corporate positions recently, but none seemed to be the right fit for you. Until now."

"This is not how I imagined being promoted."

"That makes two of us. This is definitely not how I imagined doing the promoting. One way to look at it would be to say that we're going to start fresh," he added.

Maybe he had a point. But she wasn't about to let him know that. Why let him off easy? Clearly, Cabe Jordan was used to having things handed to him merely because he asked. Unlike someone such as her who'd had to work hard all her life for every accomplishment.

A small part of her nagged that resisting might indeed be a mistake. She still needed this job, pride or not. What if he called her bluff? Her pride won out. "You have to understand, Cabe. I'm no longer sure how I feel about working for you. Given our past history as friends, and that you've known me for decades, I would have appreciated it if you'd come to me right from the start." Oh, heavens. She nearly choked on the words. For all her bravado, she had to acknowledge that he'd genuinely and wholly hurt her. She'd been foolish to expect any more from the Jordan CEO, regardless of past friendship.

But then Cabe held both hands up in surrender and she had a split second of panic. For all her bravado, she really would prefer to be gainfully employed as she looked for another position. Her breath held while he spoke.

"Let's compromise. You just help me on this one overseas project. We'll start from there."

"And then what?"

"Then we revisit the situation and the matter of your employment."

She gave her head a small shake. "You're going to have to be more specific."

"I just mean that I don't think you should make any lasting decisions right now, in the heat of the moment."

Jenna's phone rang but she ignored it, unable to tear her eyes away from Cabe's intense, steel-blue gaze. "We don't want to be impulsive."

She decided to give in just a little. "Perhaps we don't."

Cabe pounced, assuming success. "Do you have a valid passport? If not, we can request rush processing and you can meet me there once it arrives."

She raised an eyebrow. "Cabe?"

"Yes?"

"Do you actually know the definition of *impulsive*?"

Her question gave him pause, and then he laughed. "I see your point. Nevertheless."

"I have a current passport."

"Great. It's settled, then."

She stood, met him eye to eye. "Not so fast, Cabe."

Was that a smile still on his lips? He couldn't be enjoying this. "Before I say yes, I have a stipulation."

"What's that?"

"Once the new site is opened, upon completion of this project, I want a glowing recommendation from you. In case I decide to look for a position elsewhere."

"I hardly think that will be ne—"

She cut him off. "It's nonnegotiable. I want your word that you will assist me if I decide to leave Jordan's Fine Jewelry." It was the least he could do. After all the long hours of blood, sweat and tears that she'd put into this company. After the way he'd just treated her. And for all the work she was about to put in on this project. He owed her at least that much.

He merely nodded. "If, at the end, a recommendation is still what you want then I will give you one."

"It will be."

He crossed his arms in front of his chest and gave her a wide smile, the kind of smile that would have had her swooning if they were still in high school. Even now, her knees grew weak.

"Not if I change your mind."

CHAPTER THREE

JENNA TOWNSEND HAD clearly never been on a private jet before. Cabe guided her into the cabin and tried not to react to *her* reaction, though he had a comical urge to gently nudge her mouth closed. Instead, he patiently waited as she took small, hesitant steps up the stairs and into the aisle.

Unfortunately, there remained an awkward tension between them. In the interest of business, he chose to ignore it. She thought she might be looking for another job after the Caribbean project when it was completed. He had other ideas.

Well, he'd deal with that scenario if it happened. He'd been watching Jenna in action since he'd arrived in Boston and he had very different plans for her. He was not about to let her go anytime soon.

Now she stood in front of him, taking in her surroundings as they entered the aircraft. Cabe let her take her time.

As far as private planes went, his wasn't terribly extravagant. Pretty much standard issue. Leather seats, a mahogany table so that he could get some work done. In fact, his only indulgence had been the fully stocked bar.

"Jenna, please, have a seat." Cabe gently guided her toward one of the leather chairs and waited until she was seated before sitting down himself.

She immediately clicked on her seat belt and tightened it. She appeared to be more than merely awed. She seemed apprehensive, downright uncomfortable.

"Are you okay with flying, Jenna?" He knew she'd been on business trips before. So what was making her so jittery now?

The smile she gave him was strained, almost shy. "Mostly. I have to admit, flying is a bit of a new experience for me. We didn't travel much when I was a child." She glanced around at her surroundings. "And as far as flying in something like this…"

"It's just more convenient than flying commercial, that's all."

She let out a small laugh. "Right. Convenient."

Something he couldn't name tingled inside him. In so many ways, Jenna's reaction to his aircraft was refreshing. How many countless women had flown with him privately over the years? None of them had even seemed to notice the lavishness around them. Every one of them had taken for granted that they'd be arriving at their destination in the lap of luxury.

Ironically, rather than making him feel smug, her genuine awed reaction made him feel petty. Hadn't he been taking it all for granted himself? But he knew better than anyone that money couldn't fix everything.

He cleared his throat somewhat awkwardly as they both settled into their seats.

The flight attendant appeared momentarily. Cabe almost groaned out loud. This particular one could be quite the flirt. Normally, he let it slide and tolerated her suggestive comments. For some reason, he really wasn't in the mood to deal with it today. Not with Jenna here.

"Mr. Jordan. So nice to see you again," she said, her smile wide and inviting. She barely spared a glance at Jenna. He couldn't quite remember, but thought she had been the one to slip him her personal phone number after one flight.

Why did it bother him that she would flirt again this time? What was happening to him?

He had to remind himself this was nothing more than an ordinary business trip. He was way too focused on the woman—rather, the employee—accompanying him. That would have to change. And soon.

"Is there anything I can get for you, Mr. Jordan? Anything at all?" the woman asked, her emphasis on the repeated word impossible to miss.

He turned to find Jenna staring out the window, her cheeks stained slightly pink. Dressed in a smart navy pantsuit, her hair up in another impossibly tight style. Not one tendril drifting anywhere near her face. How in the world did she get all that hair to behave? He had a crazy image of unclipping the pin that held it all together, running his fingers through her long, thick tresses. He shook it off.

"Jenna? Is there something you'd like? Some wine, perhaps?"

Jenna shook her head. "No, thank you. I don't dare drink wine. I'll fall asleep."

"Are you sure?" He glanced at his watch. "We'll be in flight for a while. You definitely have time to take a nap."

Her eyes grew wide. You'd think he'd just suggested that she fall asleep on the job. Which in a way, he guessed he had. He laughed at her shock. "Jenna, it's all right. You'll be much more productive if you're well rested."

"Why do I get the feeling that's like the pot calling the kettle black?"

He laughed and dismissed the attendant with a polite nod. The woman hesitated, clearly disappointed, before finally stepping away.

"We'll even have some time to enjoy the sights while we're out there," he added.

She gave him a small smile that sent an inexplicable surge of pleasure through his chest. "That would be nice. I've never been to the Caribbean."

"Do you like the beach?"

"Yes, of course."

"What about fireworks?"

Her eyebrows drew together. "I love fireworks. What do the two have to do with each other?"

"The resort where we're staying, the one I'm trying to establish the retail store on, has a beach party every Thursday night. Live band, plenty of food and drinks. And fireworks."

"Sounds like quite a fete."

"Today's Thursday. We should go tonight. It would be a good way to introduce you to the island's characteristic atmosphere."

She chewed her bottom lip. He watched it swell and redden and redden. *Focus.* "Cabe, I'm not sure that's such a good idea."

"Why not?"

"I feel that it would just be better if we solely stuck to the business at hand."

Cabe shifted in the chair. Jenna appeared so

tense, so anxious. He wanted to help her loosen up somehow. But he was her boss. He had to tread carefully. Given her upbringing, it was no wonder Jenna seemed unable to relax and just enjoy life once in a while.

He couldn't blame her. Maybe he was the flip side of the same coin.

He wanted to tell her there was no reason to be so uptight around him. He wanted to show her how to relax. His motives were pure and simple. Perhaps that would make her rethink her decision to eventually leave the company. She didn't have to constantly toil to get ahead. He wanted her to see that.

Work hard. Play hard. She definitely seemed to have the first part down. He knew for a fact she'd stayed very late at the office last night finishing up last-minute details she didn't want to delegate before leaving.

"I get the sense you don't take many vacations."

"Well, I told you about that jewelry designers' conference in San Diego."

"That was a business trip, Jenna. On behalf of the company."

She shrugged. "Sure. But I made time to visit the zoo one afternoon."

So maybe there was hope for her yet. She was a tough cookie, tougher to crack than any woman he'd ever dealt with. He couldn't help but think how pleasurable it would be to see her enjoy herself. She was one of those rare people who truly deserved it. Though she clearly didn't believe so. He found himself both curious and intrigued. What kind of personality would this highly accomplished, intelligent woman have developed if she'd had even the simplest of breaks in life? How much more dynamic and spirited would she be?

"I'm afraid you will have to do some social mingling while we're there," he told her.

She pursed her lips. Clearly she didn't like that concept. "How so?"

"Opening a new site requires much more than pushing paper around in an office. Much of it requires networking. The resort employees are very friendly and outgoing people; you'll be working with most of them. You don't want to appear to be the standoffish stiff suit from Corporate."

Sure, it was a bit of an exaggeration, but not exactly a lie. It *would* help to have her get to know the resort employees and the regular guests. Though pushing the matter could be very dangerous ground he was treading. He couldn't seem to help himself.

"Like going to this island party, you mean?"

"Parties are considered by most people to be fun, Jenna."

"I've never had much time for them." She tilted her head in his direction: her implication was clear. *Unlike yourself.*

He was quite aware how well-documented his social life was. "Believe it or not, most of those galas I'm photographed at have some type of business angle. Nine times out of ten, I'm not there because I want to be." And lately, each party had been more tiresome than the last. It was becoming harder and harder every time to feign a level of interest he simply didn't feel.

She raised an eyebrow. "Yes, you looked downright pained in that latest photo. The one on the yacht where you're popping open the bottle of champagne, surrounded by bikini-clad socialites. How do you stand it?" Her tone held such mock seriousness he couldn't help but laugh. Surprisingly, his laughter earned a small chuckle from her as well.

"Those photos aren't always what they seem," he responded.

Her mouth tightened into a thin line. "Well, most of the parties I've attended, I wasn't there to enjoy myself. I was there to work, serving or to clean up afterward."

"Is that how you helped pay for your education? Working at social events?" he asked. No wonder she didn't associate social events with anything remotely pleasurable. And no doubt she'd watched her mother cross the line far too many times with all sorts of partying. Jenna Townsend had never been afforded the opportunity to simply have fun and enjoy life, not even as a child.

She nodded. "One of the ways. I did all sorts of odd jobs. Mostly waitressing. The catered parties paid better than, say, waitressing at the diner." She turned back to him as the aircraft began to taxi down the runway. "Your parents were particularly generous. I worked some of those swanky backyard barbecues your mom and dad were known for. I think you were off at college by then."

Had she? She'd never been at any of the ones he'd been present at. He wouldn't have missed her.

"I would have noticed if you were there," she said, surprising him.

"You would?"

The red stain of her cheeks grew deeper. "Of course. You were a minor celebrity in school. Big man on campus."

"I guess I was a bit driven, even back then."

"That's an understatement."

"Yeah, well. It's not like I was doing it for me."

She studied him with interest. "Who else?"

Cabe shrugged. "My parents were very busy people. I figured out at a very young age that I could either get their attention by rebelling and getting into trouble. Or I could try and excel at everything. I chose the latter."

Funny, he'd never admitted that to anyone before. But he wanted Jenna to understand that what outsiders saw of his life as a teen wasn't the complete picture.

"Did you so much as ever get detention?" she asked with a sly smile.

"I think once. It wasn't my fault. I was merely at the wrong place at the wrong time."

"That happened to me a lot," she responded.

"Getting detention?"

She shook her head. "No, being at the wrong place at the wrong time."

Cabe was about to ask her to explain, but Jenna turned and looked out the window as if she'd prefer the conversation to be over.

Perhaps she was right—sometimes the past was better off left to stay there. Though he remembered those years well—all the parties his parents held that Jenna had referred to. Including memories of the first corporate outdoor luncheon he was allowed to attend. He must have been around age fifteen or so. He'd been so nervous, making sure to say all the right things and behave in all the right ways.

The Jordan Golden Boy.

He'd acquired the moniker right around that time as well, due to his stellar grades and lightning-fast skills on the basketball and tennis courts. Accomplishments he worked his behind off to achieve. All to make himself worthy of the Jordan family.

When he'd first found out that he was a Jordan in name only.

What had she gotten herself into?

Mistake. This whole trip had been a mistake. She'd been a fool to take on this assignment. She'd been a fool to think she could play in Cabe Jordan's league on her own terms.

She was only going on this trip and working on this project in order to get the achievement on her résumé. Not for some kind of working vacation. Cabe had to realize she wasn't the type to do island-wide parties.

As if traveling in his private jet weren't enough, she might have to accompany him to a lavish tropical extravaganza. With fireworks! How was she supposed to act distant and unaffected? How was she supposed to avoid falling under Cabe Jordan's spell? He was charming enough under the most innocuous of circumstances.

By the time their jet landed, Jenna still hadn't figured it out.

Cabe stood and offered her his hand. "Ready?"

Of course not. But she simply nodded and let him guide her out of the aircraft, his hand placed gently at the small of her back. She knew he was just being courteous. But his touch wreaked havoc on her senses. The man had absolutely no idea of the effect of his presence. Didn't he see how women around him practically swooned at his feet? The flight attendant being a perfect example.

Yet somehow she was supposed to ignore the way his hand on her back sent a tingle clear down to her toes. Or how he so casually vowed to "show her a good time" while here.

She nearly tripped over the last step as they disembarked.

"Are you all right?" Cabe said behind her.

"Yes, I'm fine. It's just much hotter than I'd anticipated." That was no exaggeration. A wall of heat and humidity enveloped her as they walked toward the small stucco building that housed the island's airport. Her smart, fitted suit jacket instantly clung to her skin.

"It'll get better," Cabe assured her. "The airport is always ten to fifteen degrees hotter. You'll feel more comfortable once we're closer to the beach with an ocean breeze to temper the heat."

And what was going to temper her reaction to Cabe Jordan? She'd said too much on the flight over, drifting dangerously close to "pity me" territory—something she'd sworn never to do over the years. She wasn't about to start now. Not even if Cabe's significant charm had her tongue loosening.

And what was his story? All those things he said about having to prove himself growing up. His accomplishments had seemed to come so easy to him when they were kids. Maybe that had all been an illusion. Not that it was really any of her business. Cabe was her boss.

A sleek town car awaited them outside once they were through with customs. The driver was a pleasant tall man with skin the color of mocha coffee. He kept up a steady stream of conversation with Cabe as he maneuvered the busy streets. Based on the familiarity, Jenna guessed he was Cabe's regular driver on the island.

Jenna found herself too distracted by the scenery outside to focus on their conversation. Among lush, green mountains and the majestic sight of the ocean, the roadside sat peppered with run-down, decrepit shacks. Such poverty among such beauty. On a much smaller scale, it reminded her of the way she'd grown up—the days when they weren't sure they'd be able to eat while just a few miles away stood the glamorous, ritzy grandeur of downtown Boston. Well, she'd fought tooth and nail to climb out of that bleak existence. And she was proud of it. She'd done it on her own, through hard work and discipline. Unlike her mother, who still to this day waited for the right man to come along and save her—a rich, powerful man. Well, that idea hadn't really worked out for any of them. Jenna knew better than to fall for such fantasy.

Within forty-five minutes they arrived at the resort. After the striking displays of poverty on the roads they'd just passed through, it was like entering a different world.

A guard outside a tall, metal gate pushed a button to let them through.

"You have a few minutes to freshen up," Cabe told her. "Then I'd like to show you around, particularly the shopping center attached to the resort. You can see where the new store is to be built."

"I won't need that much time," she answered, grabbing her things off the seat. "I'd like to get started as soon as we can."

He lifted his head and stared at her, as if studying some unfamiliar object. "I know we're in a bit of a time crunch but there's no need to be quite so rushed, Jenna."

She shrugged. "I'm just anxious to get going, that's all."

"Well, we're on island time now. Things always move slower down here. You may as well relax."

As if that was possible, Jenna thought, watching him remove his jacket as the car came to a stop outside the entrance. His shoulders strained against his well-fitting tailored silk shirt. Deft fingers removed his cuff links and he rolled up his sleeves to reveal toned, tanned arms. His days on the Caribbean had certainly given him a good dose of color.

She tore her gaze away. None of this was at all conducive to relaxing in any way. The driver helped her out of the car and she emerged to the light sounds of steel-drum music in the air. The aroma of exotic flowers hit her as she stepped out. They were surrounded by lush plants and thick greenery. And large colorful flowers like she'd never before seen. She wanted to run up and inhale the scent of every single one.

A tall, statuesque woman with a thick braid down her back approached them. "Mr. Jordan.

So nice to have you back," she said to Cabe with a glowing smile.

"Glad to be back, Seema," he answered. "Though I wish it were for a more pleasant reason."

Her smile wavered. "More snags?"

"I'm afraid so." He gestured toward Jenna to join them. "But this time I have some help. Meet Jenna."

Jenna put her hand out to greet the woman but she had other ideas. Jenna found herself gripped in a tight hug.

"Welcome to the Paraiso Resort. So glad to have you here, Miss Jenna."

"Please. It's just Jenna. And I'm very glad to be here." It surprised her how much she meant it. The woman's friendly warmth magnetically drew her in.

"May I show you to your rooms?" she asked them both while a bellman grabbed their bags.

"We're right behind you," Cabe said.

Jenna tried to take in her surroundings as they were led away. Paradise. She had entered paradise. A piece of pure heaven. She could hear the gentle waves in the distance. The clear crisp air refreshed her despite the muggy heat. She loved her hometown city of Boston but this was an entirely different world.

A world full of beauty. To think, she'd almost turned down the opportunity to come.

She had to admit it to herself. Cabe was right to bring her here.

Cabe let himself fall slightly behind as they walked through the resort to the hotel room area. Seema was giving Jenna a raving summary of all the resort's amenities and attractions while Jenna listened carefully. He took a deep breath, finally allowing himself to relax. The scent of the ocean, the crystal-blue sky and the characteristic local friendliness worked their usual magic and he felt the tightness in his shoulders give way little by little.

He could hear the gentle crashing of waves and the sounds of laughter coming from the beach. A small salamander darted out and ran in front of them on the path. Jenna shrieked and jumped back, clutching her chest. In the process, she barreled right into Cabe. Realizing the intruder was a small lizard, her panicked expression turned to one of amusement. She laughed out loud, prompting him to laugh with her.

Instinctively, his arms went protectively around her middle. "Close call," he said against her ear. "But you're safe."

"You didn't tell me I might be ambushed by small green creatures on this island," she admonished with a chuckle.

"I was just hoping for a chance to rescue you."

"I hardly needed rescuing," she countered. "I was just startled, that's all."

He smiled at her. "Right."

Seema gave them a curious look. With hesitation, he finally let Jenna go and they continued walking.

Life could be so simple in the Caribbean.

They were finally here. After his colossal mistake in Boston, he wasn't so sure he could pull it off. Getting Jenna here was one thing. Now he had to get the project off the ground with her help, all the while trying to convince her to stay in his employ afterward. Employees like Jenna were hard to come by. And if she left, he'd have no one but himself to blame.

She couldn't leave the company. He didn't want to have to explain her loss to his parents.

His mom and dad put a lot of faith in him, their only child. So far, he liked to think he'd done well by them and made them proud. What he'd told Jenna on the flight here was the truth. He'd had two choices as an adolescent growing up. He could gain attention through rebellion or through accomplishment. Otherwise, his parents barely seemed to know he existed. Their grief had been encompassing and powerful, as it still was to this day. He chose to be an achiever because he realized at a young age just how lucky he was.

In his position, mistakes were out of the question. He couldn't afford the luxury of making any.

He watched as Jenna rubbed the back of her neck and nodded at something Seema told her, her face squinted in concentration. Even from this distance, Cabe could tell she was processing all the information about the resort, making mental notes. She really was one of a kind.

No matter what it took, he wasn't about to lose Jenna Townsend.

CHAPTER FOUR

"WOULD YOU LIKE to walk the rest of the way along the beach?" Seema asked her with a pleasant smile.

Jenna turned to Cabe, who gave a small shrug. "It's up to you. Though you should know, your shoes will definitely get sandy," he said, pointing to her smart navy pumps.

As if she cared. Right now, Jenna could think of nothing better than to feel soft, Caribbean sand between her toes.

"Why not?"

They took a right and the pathway led them through a network of buildings, bungalow-style structures with wooden steps spiraling up to tall doorways. The sounds of the ocean grew gradually louder and soon she could see the gentle lapping of the crystal-blue water and the golden silky sand that framed it.

She felt like she was in a travel catalog, each page a new and wondrous scene of bright, colorful images. Why had she never traveled here before? Money was always tight and her student loans were the top priority, but surely she could have scrounged and scraped and somehow over time pulled it off. How had she allowed herself to miss this part of the world for her whole adult life?

Without a cloud in the sky, the sea gleamed like liquid jewelry. She wanted so badly to run in and dive under the water, fully clothed. The image made her smile. She dared a glance at Cabe. Dear Lord, he'd undone a couple of his top shirt buttons and it took all her will to look away and not stare at the revealed patch of tanned golden skin.

Seema suddenly stopped, forcing Jenna to look around her at the reason. A procession of well-dressed men and women followed a small girl in a white lace smock toward an elaborately decorated archway on the beach.

A wedding. The scene took Jenna's breath away. A small band played reggae music next to rows of wooden chairs. Four bridesmaids dressed in calf-length, silky maroon gowns made their way down the path in front of them. Instead of shoes, their feet were adorned with golden chains and sparkly gemstone jewelry. The effect was both exotic and bohemian.

Jenna couldn't help but let a small "ooh" escape her lips. The women were all so lovely.

"Would you like to stay a moment and watch?" Seema asked her.

As much as she wanted to maintain the air of the unaffected professional, she couldn't tear herself away from the scene. She glanced at Cabe, who gave her a small nod.

"Yes, please."

Right behind them came a line of four handsome, strapping young men dressed in light gray suits. Hands clasped in front of them, they walked over to the bridesmaids' sides. The band switched to a rhythmic, reggae version of "Here Comes the Bride."

Jenna's breath caught when the bride emerged from a canopy off to the side. She was downright stunning. In a long silky white dress, she moved like a surreal vision. A tiara of colorful flowers sat on the crown of her head. A collective sigh sounded from the bridal party and those in attendance as she walked down the aisle, escorted by an older gentleman with gleaming silver hair. He looked both teary-eyed and happy.

Jenna found her eyes had moistened as well. How silly of her. Why in the world was she so moved by a beachfront wedding?

It made no sense whatsoever. None.

"Jenna? Are you all right?" Cabe materialized in her line of vision. Great. Just great. She was a sniffling fool who couldn't handle the sentimentality of watching two strangers get married.

"I'm fine." She thought about lying, claiming that sand had blown in her eyes and irritated them. But something told her he would see through that. Though they'd barely known each other growing up and though he'd only been a signature at the bottom of her memos for the past few years, Cabe Jordan seemed to be able to read her very well.

"It's just that she's so beautiful. And the scene is so touching," she admitted instead. "You wouldn't understand," she added. How could he? He'd grown up with the best that life had to offer. Two parents who were still together and who took good care of him.

He looked away. "You'd be surprised."

Jenna studied him. What could that possibly mean? Why did she want so badly to find out?

Seema patted her arm. "We have a well-earned reputation for planning the most romantic and unforgettable weddings."

"They seem so in love," Jenna said, staring at the laughing couple. "So lucky to have found each other."

"Luck is a mysterious thing," she heard Cabe say.

"Do you have something against weddings?" she asked him, then felt foolish for doing so. What a nonsense question to ask your boss.

"I don't really give them a whole lot of thought"

was his reply as he turned back to them. "But they're certainly good for business. The resort caters to families as well as couples," he told her. "I've heard stories of couples traveling here to get engaged. Then returning for their wedding. And several years later, coming back with their toddlers in tow." She detected a hint of sadness in his voice. But that was silly. Surely she'd imagined it.

"And don't forget," Seema added. "When they marry here, the honeymoon immediately follows."

That was the most wonderful thing Jenna had ever heard.

"That's what this place is all about," Cabe said. "Love and family." His tone held an unmistakable tinge of something she couldn't place. Longing, perhaps? Again, just a silly thought. Cabe Jordan surely couldn't have wanted for much in his full and privileged life.

Boisterous applause from the wedding party suddenly erupted and she turned to see the bride and groom kiss each other in front of a smiling clergyman.

A profound sense of sadness overcame her as she watched the couple embrace. Everyone cheered them on. Friends, family. They were all so happy for these two people.

She could never hope to have such a happy ceremony in her own future, even if she met someone. She had no real family—only her brother, who was struggling just to get by as she was. She'd long ago given up on the hope that her mother might one day clean herself up and become the kind of woman who'd be able to help her daughter plan a wedding. That was a downright laughable thought.

She had no father figure to walk her down the aisle and tear up as he gave her away.

What did it matter? She had her life planned out. She had only herself and her brother. And that was fine. Her goals were set and clear. None of those goals included finding a mate and settling down. She'd be perfectly content with a fulfilling job and financial security. Even if she never met Mr. Right.

Her gaze traveled in Cabe's direction and she had to snap herself back. Thinking about Cabe in such a way was a slippery slope she did not want to find herself tumbling down.

Not that he was ever likely to see *her* in any kind of romantic light. She was no supermodel or high-profile actress, his usual type.

She shook off the useless thoughts. Nothing would be gained from them. She was here to do a job, not fantasize.

Still, it was hard not to imagine herself standing in front of a crystal clear ocean, under the bright blue sky, as the love of her life looked her in the eyes. Once more, an unbidden image of Cabe standing before her popped into her head and she nearly gasped out loud.

Now she had passed the boundary from fantasy into foolishness. As if.

On top of everything else, the man was a notorious womanizer.

She took a steadying breath and turned to

Seema, avoiding Cabe's eyes at all costs. "That was lovely. You certainly know what you're doing in the wedding planning department."

"Thank you. We pay attention to details and try to make sure everything is perfect."

It certainly appeared that way to her. "I'd love to see the rooms. Something tells me those will not disappoint either."

Seema tilted her head and gestured with her hand for them to follow her. "We always reserve the best rooms for Mr. Jordan and any of his guests."

And how many "guests" had he previously traveled here with? Again, a wayward thought that didn't matter.

Jenna turned to catch one last glimpse of the fairy-tale wedding. The dancing had begun, right on the beach, in the sand. The flower girl seemed to be particularly enjoying the music. She and an older woman were happily dancing in the water as waves splashed at their feet.

Jenna made herself look away. She was happy for the unknown couple. She really was. They truly did appear to be an example of the lucky few who were fortunate enough to find their soul mate. But one never knew for sure. How often had her mother been convinced she'd found "the one," only to have the whole thing fall apart and send her into another downward spiral? Too often to keep track of. Each of Amanda's relapses being usually much worse than the last.

The sounds of bottle corks popping and joyful laughter followed them as they left.

Cabe watched Jenna as they opened the door to their suite. She inhaled sharply upon stepping inside.

The resort had provided his regular suite—he'd made certain of it. Jenna would be in the adjoining room and they'd share the center living area where they could work and go over the planning and budgeting of the new store.

Seema showed Jenna to her room as Cabe took the time to sign onto the Wi-Fi and check his messages. It was clear from the snippets of conversation he could hear that the two women were becoming fast friends. He wasn't surprised. Jenna seemed to be one of those rare authentic and open people who drew others in. She didn't even realize she was doing it.

When Seema bade them both goodbye several minutes later, Jenna wasted no time in getting to work. She hadn't even slipped off her shoes.

"Do you want to go over the project plan?" she asked.

"Why don't you freshen up first? Can I pour you a glass of wine? Then maybe we can grab a bite. The Hibachi restaurant on the premises is world-renowned."

She seemed perplexed by the question. He really had to figure out a way to get her to loosen up. People so often accused him of being a workaholic. Jenna Townsend could give him a run for his money any day.

He really wanted to change that. But he really didn't want to examine why.

"Wine? Now? With you?"

From the look on her face and the incredulous voice, you'd think he'd asked her to go streaking through Boston Common in the middle of a Saturday afternoon. "Or we could have soda. Or some juice."

She shook her head. "I'm not thirsty."

"Jenna, that's a lie. How can you not be thirsty? Or hungry? We've been traveling all day."

She swallowed. "If it's all the same to you, I'd rather just go over some of the to-do items for this trip and then call it a day."

Disappointment washed over him. The soft, affected woman who'd gone teary-eyed watching the beach wedding was nowhere in sight now. He couldn't help but feel it had something to do with him. Jenna Townsend turned into the stony, consummate professional whenever they were alone.

He pointed to the clock above the mantel. "It's five-thirty. We gained an hour due to the time change. There's still hours of daylight left. You'll be miserable if you don't fight through the jet lag and adjust to the new time."

Silence.

He sighed. "Jenna, look. It's been a tiring day. I don't know how productive we're going to be on an empty stomach after such a long trip. Sure, we can go over some paperwork. I think that's a great idea. But I'm going to have a glass of the resort's house Cabernet while we do so. I'd highly recommend it—it's spicy yet smooth with a hint of citrus. But of course, you can drink whatever you'd like. After which, I'd like to grab a bite of dinner, preferably at the Hibachi restaurant. I'd love for you to join me."

"It hardly sounds productive."

"You can't be productive if you're starving."

She pursed her lips. Most things with her seemed to require a fight but he couldn't help but admire her tenacity. "This is no different than a working dinner that we may have had back in Boston. How about after dinner, we tour the mall where the new store is supposed to go. It's in an adjacent building to the restaurant. Everything is connected here."

She lifted her chin. "I suppose that makes sense. But…"

At least she was giving it some thought. Cabe realized he was holding his breath. He'd been on this resort countless times, both with and without companionship. Carmen had joined him just last month, lounging by the pool or on the beach during the day and then joining him for an evening meal and entertainment afterward.

But he'd also dined alone here on numerous occasions. The friendly staff being so accommodating and social, eating by himself had never bothered him.

Yet he found he really didn't want a solitary meal tonight. He wanted Jenna's company. He wanted to ask her how hard it had been to go to business school given all her responsibilities and lack of support. He wanted to talk to her about why she was so hesitant to let her guard down. He wanted to ask her about her brother. How hard had it been to put herself through school? He wanted to learn so much more about her. It would probably be the most interesting conversation he'd had with someone in ages.

Maybe it was all those years growing up that he'd had to eat his dinners alone, his parents either too busy or preferring to eat an "adult meal" by themselves. Maybe it was all catching up with him for some reason.

"But you have a different idea, I'm guessing," he said.

She lifted an eyebrow. "As a matter of fact, I do."

He waited.

"We go over the files while I have a cup of tea. And then we visit the mall. Before dinner. So that while we eat you can familiarize me with the logistics and the details."

He groaned and rubbed his stomach with mock exaggeration. She visibly fought hard to control it but an amused smile touched her lips. "As much as my hungry stomach protests…" He stood and extended his hand. "Deal."

Her smile turned to one of satisfaction and she reached for his hand to shake it. Her hand felt small in his, her skin soft. Cabe found himself not wanting to let go, silly as the notion was. Was her skin that soft, that smooth all over?

"Great. You grab a tea bag while I pour myself

some wine," he said, finally dropping her hand. What in the world had come over him?

She turned to do so. Her smart, sensible pumps clicking on the tile.

Three hours later, after a tour of the mall and a very entertaining dinner, they made their way back toward their suite by way of the beach. The picnic tables were already filling up for the evening's festivities. Buffet tables lined with desserts, fruit and beverages framed the sitting area. All of it faced a makeshift dance floor with large speakers on either side.

"This is the big party?" Jenna asked, slowing her stride.

Cabe nodded. "Takes them a while to set up. I can drop you off back at the room and come back once it's in full swing."

Though the thought of coming back alone didn't exactly appeal to him. The last one of these he'd attended, Carmen had accompanied him. His feet hurt just thinking about it. The woman had an insatiable desire to dance the night away; no amount of partying seemed to be enough. He'd barely gotten a chance to sit all evening.

He wanted to experience the party through Jenna's fresh eyes. No doubt she'd be impressed if she just gave it a chance.

He was debating the wisdom of asking her again when they were interrupted by the sound of feminine laughter. Seema ran up to them, flashing a delighted smile.

"Jenna! I'm so glad you've come to our grand gala," she exclaimed and gave Jenna's shoulders a squeeze.

"Oh, I'm not—" The woman didn't give Jenna a chance to complete the protest. She took her by the elbow and guided her toward the middle of the action, closer to the speakers and dance floor. Jenna had changed into a flowing summery dress that clung to her in all the right places. But with her hair still up in that tight ponytail, she hadn't lost the look of the serious professional. Though at the moment she looked quite uncertain.

Cabe gave her an apologetic shrug when she glanced back at him.

By the time he reached the two women, Jenna was tapping her toe in tune with the music, swaying slightly with the beat. Midway through the song, Seema excused herself when a young gentleman asked her to dance.

Jenna laughed out loud when the young man twirled Seema onto the dance floor.

"Can I dare to say that you might be finding this enjoyable?" Cabe asked.

Jenna ducked her head but not before he caught the small smile. "It does seem very festive. And the music is very catchy."

He lifted a fresh coconut speared with a straw off one of the tables and reached it out to her.

She shook her head and put a hand on her midsection. "No way. I'm still full from dinner."

He handed her the drink. "Just one sip. You've never tasted coconut water unless you've had it straight from the fruit."

She scanned his face then finally leaned over to take a sip while he held the fruit out to her.

When she lifted her head, a tiny drop glistened at the bottom of her lip. For an insane moment, he wanted to reach out and wipe it away with his finger. Sanity won out and his hand tightened into a fist at his side. He pointed at her mouth instead.

"You just have a little…"

"Oh!" she exclaimed and wiped it away with the back of her hand.

"Well? What do you think? Better than the supermarket bottled kind?"

"It's heavenly. I wish I hadn't eaten so much."

"We'll make sure you get one tomorrow."

He went to take his own sip and her eyes grew wide. He'd shocked her, using the same straw she'd just had her lips on. Surprisingly, he hadn't even thought about it. A boss and his employee could drink from the same straw, couldn't they? Though he'd be hard-pressed to think of any other employee he'd ever done such a thing with. Plus, he had to admit, anyone watching them right now might get a different idea about who exactly they were to each other.

A look around suggested as much. The usual staffers he'd come to know gave them curious glances. He should have announced more widely that he'd be bringing a colleague with him this time around. The last thing he or Jenna needed was a swell of gossip as they were trying to get this project off the ground. If things went as planned, Jenna would spend a lot of time here working with these very people. He didn't want to impact their impression of her before they'd even had a chance to form one.

And he certainly didn't need her to be viewed as the boss's toy.

He was straddling a fine line here. He had to be careful not to step over the edge.

"All right. You win," she said with a small sigh.

"Win?"

"I have to admit, this is quite a party. I'm glad I didn't miss it."

He felt a surge of pleasure clear to his toes. How juvenile, but he was ridiculously happy that she was enjoying herself. Finally. To the point where she felt compelled to admit it.

"I would say I told you so…"

She laughed out loud, a mesmerizing, melodic

sound that made him chuckle in return. Something about the sound of her laughter made him want to join in her merriment. "And you essentially just have," she told him.

"Do I appear smug?"

She pinched the fingers of her right hand. "Just a smidge."

"Well, forgive me. But do you know what it took to get you out here? Worse than negotiating a store lease agreement. It was quite a challenge, I must say."

Her smile widened. "Yet another one that you've met and conquered."

"Was that a compliment? Or a dig? Somewhat hard to tell."

She shrugged, watched as a gaggle of dancing teenagers pranced by them. "Merely a statement."

He took another sip of the coconut drink. "Pity. I was hoping for the former."

"Fishing for compliments, are you?"

"My ego is a fragile thing." He held his hand to his chest with mock melodrama.

That laugh again—he could easily get used

to it. "Something tells me you come by compliments quite often," she said.

He took a moment to respond, deciding to throw caution to the wind. "Some compliments mean more than others, given the source."

She sucked in a breath. He wanted to suck the words back as soon as they'd left his lips. Jenna wasn't some new acquaintance; he knew better than to sound even remotely flirtatious. Where had that statement even come from?

They stood side by side now, the party growing ever larger around them, the crowd gradually becoming louder. Cabe waited apprehensively for her response. When she finally did, it wasn't at all what he was expecting.

"I'm sorry," she said.

"Whatever for?"

"My comment was a bit personal. Inappropriately so, I'm afraid."

A jarring sense of disappointment settled in his gut. Jenna was pulling the curtain of propriety between them. She was right to do so, of course. He was the one being foolish enough to let it bother him.

He turned to face her, though she remained in place and continued to look straight ahead. Definitely uncomfortable. "No need to apologize, Jenna. We'll be working very closely for quite a while. You can ask me anything. Personal or not. What would you like to know?" Now he'd definitely thrown down the gauntlet. He'd never said those words to anyone else before. What was it about this woman? She was like the smoothest Caribbean rum. Or truth serum.

"What makes you think I have questions about you?"

"There's nothing you'd like to know?"

Why was he doing this? Why did he want so badly to get her to probe? But he knew the answer. For some bothersome reason he couldn't explain, he wanted Jenna Townsend to see through his outer demeanor. He wanted her to see the real man beneath the business titles and web articles.

For the first time in his life, he wanted a woman to look inside the shell that was Cabe Jordan.

He wanted her to know the truth: that he was nothing more than a fraud.

CHAPTER FIVE

HOW IN THE world had she gotten here?

Never mind the trip itself. What was she doing here at this boisterous beach party? While Cabe hand-fed her drinks, no less. Of course, she was having fun. But that was hardly the problem.

No, the problem was her reaction to the man here with her. How aware of him she was. They way her heart had pounded in her chest when he'd taken a sip off the same straw she'd used just an instant before.

Now he stood inches from her side, goading her to ask him the questions that had been tumbling around in her head. Right. Like she could ever come out and admit just how curious she was about him. Had he sensed her curiosity? Or was he just used to people being inquisitive about him?

She could swear she felt electricity crackle between them as he waited for her response. Did he feel something also?

She was a fool. Of course he didn't. He was a worldly businessman; conversations like this one certainly amounted to nothing more than small talk for someone like him. And here she was with her heart hammering, falling for his charm.

She shook her head. "I can't think of anything I'd like to ask," she lied.

He looked away but not before she caught the clear flash of disappointment in his eyes. Her heart plunged at his expression and she sucked in a deep breath. She'd clearly let him down with her response.

That was it. She couldn't stay. A few more minutes and she was out of here. She turned to tell him so just as a tall man in a silk maroon shirt and well-fitting white pants smacked a hand on Cabe's shoulder.

"So I see you're back, my friend."

Cabe turned to greet him and the two men shook hands. Cabe's smile didn't quite reach his eyes. Animosity etched his features. She had to wonder if the use of the word "friend" was a bit of a stretch, at least as far as Cabe was concerned.

The man turned to flash her a megawatt smile. "I see you have the most beautiful woman on the island at your side."

Jenna resisted the urge to mock-fan herself. Wow. What a charmer. Cabe's fake smile turned into an all-out frown.

He introduced her while the man lifted her hand and brushed his lips across her knuckles.

"Jenna, this is Maxim Rolff. He's in charge of the on-site casino."

"A true delight to meet you," Maxim said.

Maxim was elegant—tall with dark chestnut hair and a thin mustache that would look silly on most men. On him it looked regal and distinguished. She could easily see him charming vacationers to bet significant amounts of their hard-earned money, particularly the women.

"Nice to meet you," she said with a polite smile.

"Jenna is working on the store opening with me," Cabe told him.

Maxim winked. "Works with you, does she? Glad to hear it."

What was that supposed to mean?

"I hope I can assume that you'll be spending a lot of time on our little island," Maxim said.

"It looks that way."

"Superb. I'd love to show you around the gaming tables while you're here."

Cabe jammed his hands in his pockets. "She'll be pretty busy, Maxim. We have a lot to do."

"Pity. Still, she does need to get to know the resort. And the casino is no small part of it."

"I'd love to check it out sometime," she said and stole a glance at Cabe. His frown had definitely grown. She didn't think he was even trying to hide it. "If timing allows," she added.

Maxim took her hand once more, held it. "We'll make sure of it. Won't we, Cabe?"

"Like I said, we both have a lot to do."

Maxim hadn't torn his gaze off her. "Don't let him work you too hard, my dear. It would be a shame to waste such beauty without fully appreciating it."

Cabe actually snorted. "Are we still talking about the island?" His question had Jenna gasping with surprise.

Maxim laughed. "Maybe. Maybe not. So what is it exactly that you do for Cabe?"

"I'm just assisting him with the opening of the new store."

Cabe stepped closer to her side, their shoulders almost touching. If Jenna didn't know better, she'd think he was trying to slightly push her farther away from Maxim. "Modest to a fault. She's going to be my right hand on this project. By title, she's my regional manager for the New England area."

Maxim lifted an eyebrow in appraisal. "Impressive."

She could feel the heat of Cabe's skin brushing against her shoulder. "Yes, she is."

"You're lucky to have found her," Maxim added.

Jenna stiffened in shock as Cabe threw an arm around her shoulder. "Jenna and I have known each other since we were kids. We grew up in the same town."

Maxim's brows lifted. "Ah, so friends as well as colleagues."

She couldn't come up with anything to say. Cabe's stance was definitely a possessive one. All she could summon was a tight smile.

"I look forward to seeing more of you, Jenna," Maxim said. "And please, if you can steal away from your overdemanding boss, stop by my office. I'll give you the grand tour of all the gaming attractions." He lifted her hand for another kiss before turning to leave.

"Well, that was interesting," she commented as they watched Maxim walk away. Cabe kept his arm on her shoulder for another beat, then dropped it to his side.

"*Interesting* is one word for him."

She had to laugh. "Do I dare ask what other ones you have for him?"

"Sure. Cunning. Sly. He's one to keep an eye on."

"Why do you say that?"

Cabe accepted a bubbling glass of some kind of fizzy punch from a passing waiter. He offered it to her but she shook her head to decline. Taking a swig, he threw another stare at the retreating man's back.

"He's a notorious flirt. As you just witnessed."

"Some people might call that friendly," Jenna countered. "After all, the Caribbean is known for its hospitality. You said so yourself."

"That wasn't friendly. That was shameless. The way he was flirting with you so blatantly. He would have tried to sweep you off your feet if I wasn't here with you."

A silly jolt of pleasure shot through her core. If she didn't know better, she might say Cabe was acting protective. Maybe even jealous.

But that was a ridiculous notion. He clearly simply disliked the man. And he probably didn't want her distracted when she had so much to do.

That was all.

"Come on. Let's go," Cabe said, setting down his drink on a nearby table.

Finally. She was oh, so ready to retire. Her

head was spinning. Between jet lag, exhaustion and Cabe's mere proximity, her senses revved on overdrive. Plus, the party had suddenly crowded with dozens of revelers who had somehow shown up all at once when she wasn't paying attention.

But instead of leading her toward their building, Cabe took her by the arm and led her to the middle of the beach. Right toward the dance floor.

"What are you—?"

Her words were cut off when he grabbed her by the waist and pulled her into the crowd. Right into the middle of a conga line. Her knees grew wobbly. She'd never been much of a dancer.

This was a new experience, Jenna thought as she fought to get her bearings. She might have fallen forward on her face if Cabe wasn't holding her. Without any choice, she reached out and held on to the waist of the woman in front of her and tried not to grip too tight. Then she just made her feet move.

"You're not kicking," Cabe said loudly into her ear from behind.

Was he serious? It was all she could do not to stumble into the conga dancer in front of her. With Cabe's fingers splayed across her mid-section, holding her. She felt the strength in his hands, his touch warming her flesh through her dress where he held her above her hips. Even in the middle of this large and noisy crowd, his touch felt intimate, private.

Oh, Lord. She had enough trouble keeping her wits around him under the best of circumstances. Now she had to ignore his touch and try to dance at the same time.

"It's one-two-three kick and kick," he told her, shouting above the noise.

This was so not the time for a dance lesson. "I've never done this before," she yelled back over her shoulder.

"It's easy," he said, then laughed when she stumbled yet again. "You can do better than that. You're just not letting yourself."

"I'm trying not to let myself be trampled."

He laughed and she felt his warm breath against

the back of her neck. "Don't think too hard. Just relax and let go."

Hysterical laughter bubbled up inside her. Relax, he said. Right.

"I won't let you fall, Jenna."

She believed him. And surprisingly, as soon as he said the words, some of the tension left her body. Her legs started moving easier, more fluidly. She moved much smoother in the line, not disrupting it nearly as often.

Now that she was no longer horrified, she had to concede that she was actually having fun.

Her respite was short-lived. Just as she was finally synchronized with the other dancers, the music changed. The beat slowed drastically to a smooth, rhythmic reggae tune. Definitely not a conga. Almost everyone around them stopped to find a partner and began to slow-dance.

Jenna's pulse hammered. Sure enough, she turned to find Cabe watching her expectantly. She wanted to turn away, to run from him. But when he lifted his arms and beckoned, she found herself stepping into his embrace instead. He gently wrapped his arms around her, clasping his hands against her lower back.

Then Jenna promptly stepped on his foot. To his credit, Cabe didn't so much as wince. At her mortified gasp, he dipped his head toward hers. "Don't worry. You'll quickly get the hang of this, too. You're a natural."

Jenna's mind barely registered his words. He was so close, she could smell the now familiar sent of sandalwood combined with the sea salt air. The heat from his hands warmed the skin at the small of her back as he swayed with her to the music.

She should pull away, Jenna thought. Thank him politely and then just make her way off the dance floor. She really wasn't being terribly professional at the moment.

As if reading her thoughts, Cabe's hold on her tightened ever so slightly.

"Just relax. You can't dance to a slow song when you're tense," he coaxed.

She wanted to say something, anything. But her mouth had gone dry.

Surprisingly, once again her body reacted to Cabe's words. She felt some of the tension leave her muscles, and the tightness in her shoulders lessened. She leaned into him, let her head rest on his hard chest. She heard his heart beating against her ear, the steady rhythm soothing her down to her soul. She was beyond comfortable in Cabe Jordan's arms. It wasn't that preposterous. She knew Cabe. She'd known him most of her life. They'd grown up within a few short miles of each other, had roamed the same school hallways. And right now, she felt completely safe and secure in his arms.

What was happening to her? Who was this girl, dancing on a silky beach with a wildly handsome, enigmatic man she had no business being attracted to? She'd never behave in such a manner if they were back in Boston.

Or anywhere else on the planet, for that matter.

This wasn't her. Some type of island magic had turned her into someone else. The song ended and Jenna awkwardly stepped out of Cabe's embrace. A foreboding expression shuttered his face, a tic working along his jaw. Her pulse was hammering as well. Before she could think of anything appropriate to say, a beaming Seema ran up to them, holding something out to her.

"Congratulations, Jenna. You won!" Jenna looked down at the object the other woman handed her, three small gold statuettes mounted on a marble base—dancers in a conga line.

A trophy. Jenna had never been rewarded a trophy before.

"You were selected as the best conga dancer at the party," Seema exclaimed, her smile beaming.

Clearly, a sympathy win. Still, Jenna found herself inexplicably pleased.

"Wow. Thanks." She couldn't help the wayward smile that sneaked to her lips. "I've never won anything like this before. And especially not for dancing."

Seema gave her a hug before walking away.

"Nice job," Cabe told her. "Your first time and you get a trophy."

"No doubt it's for *most improved*. Still, this will look great in my office."

He studied her. "You're really excited about it, aren't you?"

She felt the flush creep into her cheeks. "You wouldn't understand. You most certainly have cases and cases full of all the trophies you've won over the years. All the athletic competitions you won."

"There were a few first-place math-club ribbons as well."

Jenna rolled her eyes with amusement. "None for modesty, I'm guessing." She rubbed her finger over one of the small statues. How silly of her to feel so touched—it was just a cheap trophy. One she didn't even really do anything to win. But she was proud of it just the same. "Like I said, you wouldn't understand."

"I'm glad it means something to you, Jenna."

"You're laughing at me. You must be, given all the real awards you've won over the years."

He shook his head. "No, I promise I'm not laughing at you. Trust me, my trophies never meant much. Not to anyone."

Something in the tone of his voice gave Jenna pause.

Cabe took a swig of his drink. "No one ever really saw me win them, after all."

"What are you talking about? The whole school witnessed you win or place most every contest." But as she said the words, an odd thought struck her—Cabe's parents had been noticeably absent at all those events. In fact, now that she really thought about it, she'd be hard-pressed to recall ever seeing James or Tricia at a single school game or play.

Despite the fact that their son had been the star at most of them.

The cursed insomnia plagued him again. Cabe tossed with annoyance onto his side in the king-size bed and noted the time on the bright digital clock. Twelve-thirty. He hadn't slept at all. Nothing unusual about that. But this was the first time it had happened in the Caribbean. Usually the combination of the heat, the long travel time and a packed agenda had him falling asleep before his head hit the pillow.

Not so this time.

Cabe knew the reason. He couldn't help but replay the events of earlier this evening repeatedly in his head: Jenna by his side as he led her through the beach party. The way she swayed to the music. Her delight at the colorful night sky as it burst in fireworks. The way she'd felt in his arms.

He'd behaved utterly unprofessionally.

Especially once Maxim had shown up and expressed a clear interest in her. He'd never been a fan of the overbearing man. But this was the first time he'd actually felt a desire to do him physical harm. And it showed.

Cabe hadn't tried hard enough to hide his animosity.

Then he'd really lost his mind. He'd taken her to the dance floor. And he hadn't let her go when the music slowed.

It was unacceptable and he couldn't let it happen again. He was treading on thin ice as it was when it came to Jenna Townsend. He couldn't seem to stop acting erratically where she was concerned. He sighed and rubbed a hand down his face.

Outside, the party was still going strong. The band, contracted for up until an hour ago, continued to play. Island time was fluid. They would quit when they felt like it. And people would dance up until they did. The night was muggy and the air conditioner wasn't quite keeping up, none of which helped his insomnia. Shirtless, with just his pajama bottoms on, he reluctantly got out of bed.

He may as well go out onto the balcony for some fresh air. Maybe it would help.

Pulling the screen door open, he stepped into the moonlit night and watched the glitter of the ocean.

Jenna's light was on next door.

Her screen door sat adjacent to his on the same balcony. Though her blinds were shut, it was obvious she was still awake. He could hear her shuffling about. Either she was a night owl or she was having trouble sleeping also.

Well, he wasn't about to ask.

He'd been careless enough with her today. The last thing he wanted to do was knock on her door in the middle of the night.

He heard more muted sounds coming from behind her screen door. What was she doing in there?

Without warning, her screen door flew open and she stepped outside with a huff. She did a double take when she saw him.

"You're awake," she observed, her eyes wide.

"And so are you."

He leaned over the banister, his arms resting on the railing. He didn't want to think too much about the formfitting tank top she wore or how it offered a tantalizing view of her shoulders, nor the thigh-length boy shorts she had on. Or how they sat low on her hips. Hips he'd had his hands on just a few short hours ago. His fingers tingled at the thought and he shook it off.

"What's keeping you up? The music? The sounds of laughter and partying?"

"None of the above," she answered. "Sorry.

You probably wanted some time alone. I'll just go back in."

Damn it. He wanted her to be more comfortable around him. She didn't have to feel like she had to dash inside just because he was out here, too.

"Jenna. We are obviously both having trouble falling asleep. I'm out here to get some fresh air. So are you. There's plenty of it for both of us. We can share our insomnia."

She halted on the threshold and pivoted back. "Okay, then. But I don't have insomnia."

"No? You could have fooled me."

"I can't sleep because I can't stop scratching. My legs in particular are in bad shape."

He glanced down. "Sand fleas."

"Is that what caused the coin-sized itchy welts all over my calves?"

He bit his lip to keep from smiling. It really wasn't funny. "I'm sorry. I should have warned you. Some people are more susceptible to them than others."

"Oh, I appear to be one of the lucky ones."

"Is it bad?"

"I'm ready to scratch my skin off."

He approached her. "Can I take a look?"

Even in the dim lighting of the half-moon, he could see her cheeks redden. "I'm sure it'll be fine. I'll just go soak in the tub or something."

She turned to step away but stopped when he leaned down to her feet. He studied her legs, trying not to notice the toned shapely flesh of her thighs and how they led up to feminine, rounded hips.

Yep, she had several angry-looking bites.

"Soaking won't help," he informed her. "The hot water might actually make it worse."

"Great. Just great."

"But you're in luck."

She gave him a look of disbelief. "Um. How so?"

"Last time I was here I had a couple of bites. Seema gave me something for them. Seemed to work really well."

"Two whole bites, huh? And I'm the lucky one?"

He laughed and motioned for her to come inside his room. "Follow me."

She hesitated. "That's okay, Cabe. I don't want to interrupt your night any longer."

There she went again. Why was she so damn timid around him? Did she think he would bite her, too? Not that the thought hadn't crossed his mind.

"There's no reason to suffer, Jenna. I'll just go get you the stuff."

Without waiting for a response, he turned and walked inside and to his bathroom. She was still waiting outside on the balcony when he returned with a tube of ointment.

He handed it to her. "This works wonders. Put a dime-sized amount on each bite. Here, I'll help you."

She looked mortified at the thought. "I can do it."

"Fine."

Taking the tube, she went to work on the numerous spots, some already on the verge of breaking open.

"It stings at first," he warned just as she let out a cry of "Ow!"

"Sorry."

Several moments later, she handed the tube back to him. "Thanks again."

He sensed her hesitation. "Is there something else?"

She looked away, off to the side. "No. Good night."

He reached out and took her by the arm to stop her as she turned on her heel.

"Jenna, what is it?"

She closed her eyes and let out a deep breath. "I feel one just below my shoulder blade. It's very itchy."

"I see. You can't reach it."

She sighed. "I've been trying to scratch it all night."

"To no avail?"

"I wouldn't ask but—"

"It's okay." He gently turned her around and lifted her ponytail up. Apparently she even slept with her hair in a cursed bow. He fought the urge to untie the ribbon and release her thick curls.

Focus. Sure enough, right above her tank's line,

she had a nasty-looking bite immediately to the bottom of her left shoulder blade.

"That one's a mosquito bite," he told her. "It appears all sorts of things are attracted to you."

Damn. Why in the world had he said that? An awkward silence fell between them before she finally broke it.

"I can't even reach it to scratch it."

"That's because you're not double-jointed." He laughed but she didn't respond. "I can't see how you're going to locate that one let alone reach it. Here, let me."

Before she could argue, he uncapped the tube and began to apply the ointment.

His breath caught as he touched her. Her skin felt warm beneath his fingers. He found himself leaning in closer. The aroma of her hair teased him, a hint of strawberries and a subtle feminine scent that was distinctly her own.

"Jenna." He whispered behind her ear, unable to help himself. His arm moved of its own accord to reach around her middle. She stiffened for the briefest of moments but then went totally lax against him. Her back against his bare chest. She felt like heaven and he knew he shouldn't be doing this. Shouldn't be holding her like this or touching her even. Hadn't he just vowed as much? But he couldn't seem to let her go. All he could do was repeat her name.

As if on cue, the clouds shifted and erased the faint moonlight they'd been bathed in. Only the dim artificial beams from the party lights in the distance afforded them any hint of respite from the dark.

"You were lying earlier, weren't you?" he found himself asking foolishly. "When you said you weren't curious about me. That you had no questions to ask."

He felt her exhale a long, deep breath. Several moments passed before she replied. "Yes," she finally admitted on a whisper.

She turned her head and his gaze fell to her lips. What would she taste like? He wanted desperately to find out.

"So do it now. Just ask me."

"I don't know, Cabe. It feels too much like gossip."

"It's okay, Jenna. We're having a conversation. That's very different."

He felt her shrug. "I can't help but see it that way. Your family has always been a source of gossip. So elevated, so unattainable."

He'd help her. "And you want to know if any of the rumors are true?"

She exhaled under his arms. "There were too many rumors to keep track of. It was more the general sense of the villagers talking as they stared at the castle."

He let out an ironic chuckle, though he felt anything but amused at the moment.

She made no effort to turn around and face him. Thankfully. Talking was so much easier this way, with her in his arms, both of them staring off at the dark shadow of the ocean in the distance.

"It was far from a castle."

His words had some kind of impact on her. She stiffened as he said it, suddenly tried to pull away.

He instinctively held on to her, didn't let her leave his arms. "What?" he asked, taken aback at her reaction.

"Says the crown prince."

He'd offended her. How could he explain it to her? Did he even want to? That what she grew up seeing was a facade. A well-crafted, expertly framed image of the perfect family. The reality had been so very different.

"It wasn't quite a fairy tale, Jenna. Please believe that." At her silence, he added, "You don't, do you?"

"You said on the beach that your trophies never meant anything. Are you trying to tell me your life was anything less than idyllic? How so? You're going to have to explain it to me. Because it sure looked that way to me and anyone else in that town."

The skepticism in her voice rang clear and loud. He swallowed, tried to gather the words.

"You know what?" Jenna said. "Never mind. Forget I asked. I only did because you told me to."

"I know. And I meant it. I'm trying to answer

in as truthful a way as possible." He took a deep breath. It was true. Something about her, maybe her strength or her openness, made him want to confide in her in a way he hadn't done with anyone else. Maybe it was the way she'd looked at him after they'd danced together on the beach. He wanted to open up more of him for her to see.

"We were supposed to appear that way," he began. "It's what we wanted everyone to see when they looked at us. Do you understand?"

She shook her head slowly, her soft silky hair skimming the stubble on his chin. "I'm afraid I don't."

"From the outside, we projected the image of the perfect little family."

"But inside the castle walls?" she prompted.

Cold. It was the first word that came to mind. Followed by *distant* and *unfeeling.* "It's hard to explain."

Her spine stiffened slightly. "Cabe, are you saying that Tricia and James were...?" She paused to take a deep breath. "That they didn't treat you well?"

Damn. She'd just jumped to the absolute wrong conclusion, that he'd been abused somehow. Physically or emotionally. That was also far from the truth. The truth sat somewhere in between.

He was really making a mess of this whole conversation. First he'd come off as the clichéd poor little rich boy. Now he'd led her to believe he'd been harmed by his very own parents. He should end this. He should just drop the whole thing and bid her a hasty good-night. But having her in his arms felt like some sort of balm. It felt right, her pressed up against him, numbing his senses. Dulling the pain.

If he stopped now, if he let her go and walked away, he'd never make his way back.

Not with Jenna. Not with anyone.

He'd never again find a way to open up about the darkness that hung over his perfect life like a heavy curtain, casting all sorts of shadows.

So he took a deep breath and just let it go. "I'm not a real Jordan, Jenna. I'm not really James and Tricia's son." The words hung thick in the air between them. Another layer pulled away from the fantasy.

What he didn't say was that his very existence was a result of his parents' greatest tragedy.

Jenna stilled. Trying to absorb what he'd just told her, no doubt. He couldn't blame her. He knew no one at school ever suspected. James and Tricia were that good at hiding the reality. And so was he.

He finally turned her around to face him, grateful for the darkness that hid what his expression must have held. "I was adopted by James and Tricia as an infant."

She lifted a shaking hand toward his chin. He resisted the urge to turn into it. "I didn't know," she offered.

"You weren't supposed to know. No one is. We moved into town when I was a preschooler. Started the business right after."

"It doesn't make you any less their son."

How many times had he heard that over the years from James and Tricia themselves? Just words. He'd always seen the truth in their eyes. The harsh reality: if they hadn't tragically lost their real son, they wouldn't have even known Cabe existed.

"Thank you for that. But it does."

She sighed, hesitated before she spoke again. "Did it bother you so terribly? Because you never showed it."

He shrugged. "The fact that I was adopted? No, that's not what bothered me."

"Other things?"

"Like I said. It's hard to explain."

"I know your father has always been very proud of you. Everyone in town knows that."

"I worked hard and made sure of it," he said. He'd tried so hard to earn their affection. He'd studied longer, played harder. Everything in his teenage power to make himself what he thought they wanted in a son. None of it was ever enough. "Still, there were those ever so rare times when I caught him staring at me," he told her.

"Staring how?"

"It's not important."

"Please tell me."

He let out a small laugh. "I don't know. He just had this look on his face, you know. A look that made me wonder and think about the reality." He'd spent his whole life trying to erase that look off his father's face. But no amount of achievement had done it so far. Nor had any of it erased the chronic, haunting sadness in his mother's eyes.

"What reality?"

The one that had shaped him since that fateful day when he'd turned fifteen, Cabe thought. That was the day the mystery fell into place just as the whole world around him crumbled. He wanted the knowledge of it off his chest, once and for all. His very heart told him that this was the moment, the chance he thought he'd never get. The woman in his arms was the key to lightening the burden. They'd grown up in such different ways but she'd be the one to understand somehow. Jenna would know what he meant when he told her that he'd been given everything he could have wanted as a child and teen. Except for one minor omission: genuine, honest parental affection.

He sucked in a breath and choked out the words. "That I would never have been their son if they'd had the choice."

"Oh, Cabe. But they did choose you," she said, her voice gentle and soothing. The situation was almost surreal, the way he was opening up to Jenna Townsend on a dark balcony in the middle of the night. Finally having the words out in the open combined with the heady way she said his name sent a surge of pure longing through him. Instinctively, he pulled her closer against him. She let out a soft moan and his gaze fell to her lips. What would they taste like? He dipped his head to find out. A mere brush of his lips against hers. Hardly a kiss at all. But it was enough to rock him straight through to his core. She sighed against his mouth and he wanted more, needed to taste her fully. He pulled her closer so that he could plunge into those lips deeper.

The band outside suddenly stopped playing and a loud cheer erupted, shattering the moment in a fast instant. The effect was like a splash of cold water. Cabe reflexively dropped his arms and for a moment they both stood frozen.

What in heaven's name was he doing?

He ran a hand through his hair. "Jenna, I shouldn't—"

Her sharp gasp cut him off. She stepped away as if struck by lightning. He almost reached for her but some small speck of sanity stopped him.

Without a word, she turned on her heel then fled into her room. He could only watch as she closed the screen door and pulled the curtain closed. In more ways than one. Her light went out an instant later.

Leaving Cabe in the dark shaking with need. And wondering what the hell he'd been thinking.

What in the world had she been thinking? She should have just turned right around and gone back into her room the second she saw Cabe out on that balcony. She'd tried but not hard enough. But then she'd never have known.

Jenna lay in bed and listened to the chirping of

the birds outside as the darkness of dawn slowly evolved into a bright sunny morning.

She hadn't slept a wink.

In a couple of short hours, she was supposed to meet Cabe for a working breakfast meeting. Calmly and professionally. She had no idea how she would pull it off. They had to address what had happened between them and everything he'd revealed.

He'd certainly dropped a bombshell on her. Cabe was not the Jordans' biological son. And he seemed very affected by it.

There had to be more to the story. For instance, why had the three of them kept the truth so under wraps? And for that matter, Cabe may have been adopted but he still seemed to have led a charmed life. But the man she'd encountered last night seemed very different than the impression she'd always had of him as the high-achieving, hand-some playboy.

His words echoed in her head. *It was supposed to look idyllic from the outside.*

He'd been drinking last night. It wasn't any

kind of excuse but it was more than what she'd had. She'd been stone-cold sober while practically melting into his arms. Oh, Lord. He'd kissed her. Well, almost. He'd touched his lips to hers and would have gone further before Jenna had found some semblance of sanity. The memory of it quickened her pulse and that just made her madder at herself.

The kiss didn't mean anything. It couldn't have. She would blame this magical location, being so far from home in such an enchanting place. So far removed from reality.

Even if Cabe was attracted to her, which he seemed to be last night, it wasn't anything to dwell on. She wasn't the type of woman Cabe Jordan was ever going to be interested in long term. They belonged on two different spheres.

Still, what he'd revealed about himself last night led her to the age-old saying: appearances could be deceiving. There was clearly more to her boss than the image she'd held for all these years. As much as Jenna had wanted to pry and get to the bottom of it all, she'd resisted. It clearly cost him to reveal as much as he had. Cabe would tell her the rest when he was ready. She would be there, available for him when he needed her.

But he pushed you away at the end.

There was that. She tossed aside the covers and got out of bed.

She was contemplating it all still two hours later after showering and getting dressed when she heard Cabe's knock.

She took a deep, fortifying breath before opening the door to greet him.

"Good morning." He didn't mean it. He looked miserable and he clearly had slept about as much as she had. Still, even with the dark circles he was utterly, heart-shatteringly handsome in his stone-gray suit and crystal-blue tie. Her mind automatically shifted to the way he'd felt last night, hard and firm against her back. She could still smell the hint of his sandalwood scent, could still feel the way his breath had felt against her cheek. The firmness of his lips as they'd touched hers.

Stop it.

She stepped aside to let him in. He didn't move

though, which surprised her. Then she saw the look on his face. Regret. He thought the whole balcony encounter was a big fiasco. A mistake. He'd probably been kicking himself all night for divulging his lifelong secret. To someone like her, no less.

"Are you ready to go?" he asked.

Jenna blinked. That was all he was going to say to her?

No hint of the gentle, open man from last night could be detected this morning. The one who'd bared his soul to her. Well, what had she expected? That he'd sweep her in his arms the moment he saw her, overwhelmed at the sight of her and all that they'd shared in the darkness?

"Do you need another minute?" he asked, glancing at his watch.

Jenna gave her head a shake. "Um, no. Let me just grab my things."

She forced a smile upon returning to the doorway. "I'm ready."

He silently turned and made his way down the stairs. Jenna stared in stunned silence before following. Now what? Did she dare say something? The awkward silence was downright unbearable. Cabe seemed in no hurry to break it. Perhaps she'd only imagined last night. Maybe it had only been a crazy dream.

No.

It had been real. She had the bug bites to prove it.

Blasted bugs. They were the reason all this was happening. If only she'd taken a moment to peer outside last night before she'd jumped out on the balcony. She would have never gone out if she'd known Cabe was there. Her legs had been itchy and stinging but no amount of balm was worth the discomfort and awkwardness of this moment.

Instinctively, she reached down and rubbed the biggest bite on the top of her thigh.

"Did the ointment not work for you?" Cabe asked, his tone brusque.

"It did. It worked great. Thank you."

"Don't mention it."

The double meaning was clear. Cabe wasn't going to bring up anything that had happened on that balcony. Nor did he want her to. The tight set of his jaw left no question about it.

Also no question that he deeply regretted it all. A brick settled in Jenna's chest. Such foolishness on her part not to see this coming. Cabe had succumbed to a moment of weakness last night. Nothing more. She'd just conveniently been there. He'd been tired, probably missing the companionship he usually had on these trips.

"I'll get you some more of it later. We have a lot to do today. We can't have you distracted. Not by itchy bites, not by anything."

Her composure almost faltered and she gritted her teeth. Subtle, he wasn't.

"I hardly feel them," she threw out. Two could play at this game.

He didn't bother to look at her. "Good."

Her eyes stung. She tried to convince herself that it was the bright early-morning sun. It was easier than facing the truth.

Just as well they'd be busy all day. The busier the better. The less time she had to think and dwell on senseless emotion, the better off she would be.

She just had to hope her highly honed focusing skills didn't let her down. It wouldn't be easy given that she'd be spending the day side by side with Cabe. After a night where she'd done nothing but toss and turn and think about him and what they'd shared.

All of which Cabe was telling her to forget.

CHAPTER SIX

CABE WANTED TO hit something. An hour spent in the resort's gym at the break of dawn followed by a two-mile jog along the beach had done nothing to ebb his agitation or his anger at himself.

Jenna knew the truth. There was no turning back on that now. At some point he had to acknowledge it. Just not now.

Of all the asinine, idiotic—

"Is something wrong?" Jenna asked him as they reached the podium where the maître d' greeted them with a smile.

He realized he'd cursed out loud. "I was just saying, this is the main dining area of the resort. Vacationers can eat here at any time of day."

She studied him with clear doubt. "Oh, really? Is that what you were saying?"

He didn't respond as they were seated. Their

table sat poolside and faced the beach, affording them a perfect view of a clear and sunny horizon. A waiter immediately greeted them and poured steaming hot coffee into two porcelain cups. A moment later, he brought out a tray of assorted pastries and platters of eggs and crispy potatoes.

They went to work right away, going over the numerous to-dos that would lead to the opening of the new store. Jenna impressed him repeatedly with her knowledge and insight. Not to mention her ability to offer solutions to matters that would have taken him twice as long to figure out by himself. Though he had numerous people working on the endeavor both in New York and on the island, he found it invaluable to have another mind just to help him with the sheer volume of details involved. He couldn't have chosen better than Jenna.

They made quite a team.

A team he couldn't risk jeopardizing again by doing anything foolish or reckless. The way he had last night. What had he done? How impulsive of him, how uncharacteristic. An unbidden image of her leaning back against him invaded his mind. He shoved it out of his head.

An hour and a half later, when the dishes had been cleared and the coffee carafe was empty, Cabe felt more in control about the opening than he had in weeks. They both had clear agendas—with phone calls to make and emails to send out.

To her credit, Jenna was staying mum about last night and giving him time to bring up the matter himself if he chose to. She apparently could tell that he was in no mood to deal with the fallout of his revelations. Once Jenna took her last sip of coffee, he stood and pulled out her chair. "Follow me. We can head to the business center and get some work done there before our meeting with the resort's retail manager this afternoon."

She had her hair up again this morning, this time in some kind of tight bun. But it was no match for the Caribbean's morning heat and humidity. A few tendrils had escaped their confines, forming wispy curls around her temples. The few short hours of daylight she'd spent here yesterday had somehow already resulted in a hint of red color across her cheeks and on the bridge of her nose. The effect was a subtle beauty that no amount of store-bought makeup could have achieved.

He stopped short. Not this again. What the devil was he doing? He had no business noticing the added color on her cheeks. Or anything about her looks, for that matter.

He couldn't even blame it on punch this time.

"Do you need to stop at your room for anything?" he asked. "It's on the way."

"No. I have everything I need."

Several children frolicked in the pool while their moms relaxed on lounge chairs reading magazines or the latest bestseller. A squealing wet toddler darted past them toward the kiddie sprinklers with his father fast on his heels. The man caught the child in a hug and carried him the rest of the way, despite the toddler's squirmy efforts to be let down.

They reached the concrete path where the resort grounds met the sandy beach. They hadn't gone far when Cabe realized Jenna had stopped.

He turned to find her staring off to the side, her hand cupped over her face to shield her eyes from the blare of the sun.

"Jenna?"

He followed her line of vision to where a young local girl sat, a variety of handcrafted items set up on display on a folding table in front of her. The resort was pretty accommodating about locals who tried to sell various wares on the property. This one had gotten here relatively early.

"Do you know what she's selling?" Jenna asked.

"Looks mostly like beaded jewelry of some sort. Maybe some leather items."

"She looks very young."

He had to agree. The girl couldn't be more than thirteen or so.

"Shouldn't she be in school?" Jenna asked.

"They're pretty relaxed about school here sometimes." She hadn't torn her gaze away from the girl. "Fridays are a good day to set up shop on the beach. A lot of tourists are either coming or going. Those arriving have their wallets still conveniently in their pockets. And the ones departing are often looking to buy last-minute souvenirs."

"I see."

"She probably had to choose between going to school or helping to feed her family for the week."

Jenna seemed torn and took a hesitant step in the girl's direction. Cabe doubted she even realized having done so. "I know we have a lot to do…" she began.

"Would you like to go take a look at the items?" he asked, unnecessarily as the answer was obvious.

He led the way without waiting for a response. "Let's go." She was fast on his heels.

The young girl's eyes lit up as they approached. Two well-dressed interested tourists was always a welcome sight.

"May I take a look?" Jenna asked.

She trailed her hand along the items and picked one up, some kind of leather necklace with colorful beads.

"This one would look so pretty with your hair color," the girl stated with a Creole accent.

"It's beautiful."

Not wasting a second, she came around the table and hung the necklace around Jenna's neck, then held up a mirror.

She turned to Cabe. "You should buy it. For your lady."

Jenna corrected her right away. "Oh, no. He's not... He won't be buying it."

The girl's face fell but she wasn't ready to quit. "You look amazing wearing it, miss." She held the mirror up higher. "See how pretty."

"I know," Jenna blurted out then blushed. "I mean, I like it. I will buy it myself."

She glanced down at the table. "Actually, I think I'll buy everything on this tray."

The girl's eyes grew wide. "Did you just say you want all of this?"

Jenna nodded and smiled. "Yes, please. I'll take that tray, everything on it."

Cabe looked down. The tray consisted of at least twenty items. Mostly necklaces made of beads. A few bracelets made of braided rubber bands. Was one of those a dog leash? Jenna didn't even care what she was buying.

That was probably more than the girl typically sold in a month. Maybe even six months.

"And a couple of those slippers," Jenna added, pointing to a pile of rubber flip-flops under the table. She hadn't even asked the price. Or size.

The girl still hadn't recovered. She stood staring at them both with a stunned expression. "You are joking? Yes?"

Jenna vehemently shook her head. "No. No joking. I'll come right back with my wallet." She turned to him. "Cabe, will you wait here? I'll be right back."

Before she could turn around, Cabe stopped her with a hand on her arm. "Stay here." He pulled out his wallet, yanked out several bills and handed them to the girl. "We'll take the whole table."

The girl audibly gasped, hesitantly taking the bills, as if Cabe might change his mind any second. Then she sprang toward Jenna, wrapping her in a big, tight hug. "Thank you. Thank you both. So very much."

She pocketed the bills and pulled out several large plastic bags, filling them with the items off her table.

Jenna turned to him with her mouth agape. "What? Why? I could have paid for the things I wanted."

"Consider it a business expense."

"How in the world would such purchases be considered a business expense?"

"Well, for one thing, they're handcrafted jewelry pieces. We're in the jewelry business. Who knows? Maybe it will give us ideas about trends and designs." Not bad for an off-the-cuff response. He was pretty impressed with himself for coming up with that one on the spot.

She pursed her lips. "You didn't need to do that. It was totally unnecessary."

He took the bags the still-grinning girl handed to them and motioned for Jenna to go forward. He could hear the young girl humming a happy Marley tune as she folded up her empty table.

"It wasn't as if you actually *wanted* any of it," he argued. "You were just trying to help the child. You can't deny that."

She lifted her chin. "As a matter of fact, I was buying souvenirs for the personnel in the Boston regional office."

"Is that so? You were going to buy the whole tray."

"My staff works hard. They deserve to be rewarded for it."

"Well, now you can reward the whole building."

"Be that as it may, you didn't have to step in and cover it all for me."

He didn't break his stride. The truth of it was, he could tell Jenna was moved by the girl's plight. And he'd merely reacted to the look in Jenna's eyes when she'd looked at the girl. Then he'd actually felt a sense of shame about all the times he'd seen that very same child set up on the beach and never thought to help her out by buying anything. When he compared that to Jenna's reaction, what did that say about him?

He'd been brought up better than that.

"Are you angry?" he asked Jenna when she'd stayed silent for several steps.

She took a deep breath. "I don't know."

Her honesty gave him pause. The females in his life usually decided right away when they were cross with him and they made sure to let him know.

He sighed. "Don't be. All that matters is we made that girl's life just a little easier. You can't argue with that."

She rubbed a hand over her eyes. "I guess not. I guess I should be thanking you instead. What you did was very generous."

"She has you to thank."

"You purchased her entire table!"

"You're the only reason we went over to her table in the first place."

Jenna looked away with a small shrug. "I wish I could do more for her. She so reminds me of—" She caught herself before she went any further with the statement. He knew what she'd been about to say. The girl reminded Jenna of herself.

The Townsend kids hadn't exactly had an easy time growing up, a fact the whole town had been aware of. He wondered how many times during their adolescence Jenna and her brother had struggled to get by. How often had Jenna spent her paycheck on groceries rather than the frivolous knickknacks most teenage girls spent their money on?

They'd reached a somewhat empty area of the beachfront. Only a handful of suntanning tourists dotted the sand and a couple of kids building a simple yet muddy sandcastle. He'd deliberately taken her this route, hoping it would settle her thoughts.

She'd had quite the forty-eight hours.

"Who knows?" he added. "Maybe once the store is opened, we'll have her or other vendors set up a booth or something inside. We'll do the high-end stuff while displaying the local ware."

She suddenly stopped in her tracks and turned to him, forcing him to stop as well. "You would do that?"

"Why not? Don't you think it's a good idea?"

She smiled up at him then. A true smile unlike he'd seen from her before. And a strange feeling unfolded in his chest, one he couldn't name.

"I think it's the most wonderful idea."

"We could establish a whole program around it. Local craft jewelry being sold along our expensive deluxe pieces." Wow, he was getting really good at coming up with all sorts of ideas right on the spot, completely off the top of his head. He had no one but Jenna to thank for it.

She touched his forearm, clearly pleased. "Oh, Cabe. I think that could really work."

"Of course it will work. And it will please the local authorities. It's a win-win." He stopped to face her. "As a matter of fact, I think you may have helped with our zoning issues. The local brass always appreciate when any new business expands community ties."

Her eyes grew wide. "But I didn't do anything. You came up with the idea yourself. You're the one who can implement it."

None of it would have even occurred to him if she hadn't been by his side. "Not so. My project manager can also implement it. I might put her in charge of the program entirely. If she's interested."

The mild touch on his arm turned to an all-out grip. "Of course I'd be interested. I know firsthand how opportunities like that can make a monumental impact on someone's life." She literally bit down on her lip after she'd said the words.

"Is that right, Jenna?"

She looked off at the horizon, her eyes growing distant and pensive. Several moments passed in silence and Cabe didn't think she would answer. Finally, she took a deep breath. "When you said she was probably out there so that she could feed her family…"

"Yes?"

She clearly struggled to find the right words. "There were plenty of nights when my brother and I didn't eat," she confessed. "Especially during the summers when there was no school lunch to fall back on. I felt responsible when he was hungry."

So unfair, Cabe thought. Jenna had been forced

to parent not only herself but also her older brother. "You were just a kid yourself."

"But he was the confused teenage boy. He looked to me for answers. Who else was there? Things got better as I grew older. Once I could start working, I made sure we both had at least one square meal a day. The elderly store owner on the corner of Falmouth and Main, down the street from our apartment, he offered me my first job. He knew I needed it. I never forgot that. Or his kindness. That man made all the difference in our lives."

"What about your mother?"

Her lips formed a grim smile. "My mother wasn't around much."

"Still. She must have had some source of income."

Jenna didn't tear her gaze off the horizon. "She mostly lived off her boyfriends. In between men, she had odd jobs. Waitressing on and off. Cleaning offices here and there. Nothing really stuck. And she had other ideas about what to do with the little income she did earn."

"Others must have helped you along the way." He sincerely hoped so. Or what did that say about the town he'd grown up in?

"Of course they did. But once I started to earn it, then it wasn't charity. It was accomplishment."

He felt the breath leave his lungs in a whoosh. Even at such a young age, Jenna Townsend had valued her pride. While he'd been out pursuing tennis trophies and merit ribbons to prove himself to his parents, she'd been fighting for survival. And she hadn't even done it for selfish reasons. She'd done it for her brother. To make sure they ate.

He didn't know what to say to her. His own struggles in life seemed to pale in comparison. Cabe had never wanted for anything. Not for anything materialistic, anyway. Sure, he'd spent most of his hours alone, his parents completely absent or completely disconnected if they were around. But the thought of going hungry was an absolute foreign concept.

"You've achieved a lot, Jenna. You're a successful, accomplished businesswoman."

A false and bitter laugh escaped her lips. "I had no choice. I had to work harder and be smarter than everyone else. I promised myself I would never be like her."

No wonder she was so driven, so rigid. Like that young vendor, Jenna had been carrying around a heavy burden since she was barely a teen. It all made sense now. Her inability to relax, her workaholic tendencies. All to outrun a legacy she'd already left so far behind. Yet somehow, it still chased her.

He and Jenna Townsend had a lot in common.

Jenna swiveled around in a large leather chair in one of the cubicles in the business center where she and Cabe had been working for the past two hours. Well, she'd been trying to work, anyway. She hadn't really gotten as much done as she would have liked. The scene from this morning kept playing over and over in her head.

Cabe hadn't even thought twice about offering that lovely girl whatever he'd had in his wallet. Sure, he could afford it. But not every wealthy man would have done the same thing. And his idea to have crafters set up in the store, that would be a true way to give back to this wonderful community she'd already grown so fond of in her short time here. Not only had he helped the girl with her immediate concern, he'd figured out a way to help her long term. All in all, a very monumental gesture.

So why did she feel so unsettled? She'd been tense and uneasy since the whole encounter. Something about the way Cabe had stepped in, taken charge of the situation, and gone above and beyond what she had intended.

It had impressed her. His kind gesture had impressed her.

And she didn't like it.

She didn't need any kind of white-knight hero to take over for her in such a situation. Hadn't that been exactly the kind of thing that would have impressed someone like her mother? Amanda loved it when the men she was with took care of things for her. Especially if the gesture involved a display of wealth.

But Cabe's actions had been all about kindness. Then he'd gone further to come up with an idea about how to continue the kindness on a broader scale.

It would be utterly selfish of Jenna to be cross with him. After all, it wasn't the use of his money that had impressed her, it was the use of his heart, his generosity. He had helped that girl more than Jenna would have been able to. So now she was an annoying bundle of frustration, anxiety and anger. Not to mention confused.

She'd spent her life ensuring that she could stand on her own two feet, that she didn't need any kind of assistance or guidance from a man the way her mom did. Cabe's take-charge personality was now blurring that previously solid image of herself she'd worked so hard to achieve.

Yep. Cabe Jordan was totally, overwhelmingly confusing her. The man was a complete enigma, impossible to comprehend. He'd opened up to her about a monumental part of his life—that he'd been adopted. But then he'd refused to even mention it again the next day. Then just when she

thought she'd imagined his openness and vulner-
ability, he'd gone ahead and made the wishes of
a needy girl come true right before Jenna's very
eyes.

Basically, he'd walked into her office a few
short days ago and completely scrambled her
senses. She had no idea how to handle him. Nor
could she imagine what her life was going to
feel like when she went back to it without him
in it. Once Cabe returned to Manhattan and she
was back in Boston, her life would never be the
same again.

But she'd have to accompany him back here to
the resort at least once or twice more before the
project was completed. Wouldn't she? Not only
was she his project manager for the store opening, she'd just been recruited for the local vendor
outreach idea.

The thought of returning both excited and ter-
rified her. Her psyche might not be able to handle another trip like this one.

She could not fall for Cabe Jordan. He was absolutely wrong for her. Look how much he'd dis-

rupted her life in the few short days since he'd stepped into it. Who was she kidding, anyway? As if he would even entertain the thought of the two of them in any kind of serious relationship. Haughty models and bright-eyed actresses were far more his style. Technically, he was dating one now.

As if her thoughts had conjured him, he materialized in front of her. His shirtsleeves were rolled up to reveal tan, muscular forearms. The man looked like he'd stepped right out of a male trends magazine. Though that was the kind of thing she did not need to be noticing.

"Late-morning doldrums?" he asked, holding out a sweaty plastic cup of iced tea. "Freshly brewed. Thought you might need a break."

Well, his timing was certainly a point in his favor. She inhaled the scent of the aromatic, lemony brew and felt her senses sharpen before she even took a sip. "Hmm, perfect. Thank you."

"You're welcome. Can't be too long a break though."

"Wow, and you said you weren't a harsh boss."

"Demanding versus harsh. Big difference. We have that meeting with the retail manager."

She turned to check the small bar on top of her laptop screen that read the date and time. "It's not for another two hours. You said we're meeting him right here on-site."

"True, but you might want to change first."

"Change? Why?"

"I meant to mention, Sonny likes to hold his meetings in an open cabana on the beach. You'll be way too warm in that pantsuit."

A business meeting in a beachside cabana. She could really get used to this lifestyle. It did pose a problem, however. All she'd really packed were other suits. Well, except for her tankini in case she had time for a swim in the ocean. That would hardly be appropriate for a meeting, even in this environment.

"Oh, dear." She looked down at her outfit.

"What's wrong?"

"I didn't really pack anything much different than what I'm wearing."

He narrowed his eyes in disbelief. "Really? All you packed are business suits and one sundress?"

He remembered her dress? He didn't seem the type to make note of such things.

She nodded, an embarrassed flush warming up her cheeks. How foolish of her. She didn't even know how to pack for a business trip. "And a swimsuit."

He seemed to think for a minute then turned abruptly. "Okay, let's go."

She knew he was a man used to being in charge and having others jump to fulfill his every demand, but these sudden turns were a bit tough to get used to. "Where exactly are we going? Two hours before our meeting?"

"The adjacent shopping center. I can check the status of the new paneling they're to start putting in today."

"Okay. What will I be doing?"

"You're going to visit the ladies' boutique. There's got to be a couple of outfits you can pick out that are more suitable for an outdoor conference."

She hadn't seen that coming. "You want me to go shopping? Now?" She gestured to the piles of paperwork on the desk and her laptop blinking with several new emails. "I don't have to remind you about all the work that needs to get done. Oh, and we have a meeting very soon."

"Well, I'm not saying you should take all day. Just go pick out a couple of things." He seemed to contemplate her, looked her up and down. "You don't strike me as one of those women who takes forever and tries on a hundred outfits."

She huffed out an exasperated sigh. "No. Of course not." She was never indecisive about clothes. She just couldn't usually afford to buy anything that wasn't marked down and finding adequate, comfortable items on sale took a bit more time. She couldn't be one of those women who shopped indiscriminately.

"Then I don't see a problem. But we're wasting time. Let's go."

"I need to get my purse from the suite."

"Why?"

Was he being deliberately obtuse? "Because you're making me shop."

"Just have them put it on my account."

Jenna halted. Oh, no. Not again. He was oh, so ready to buy things for her. The thought sent an irritated bristle up her spine. After all, this was no way comparable to the way he'd helped that girl on the beach. This was totally different. She wouldn't have it.

"You are not buying me clothes, Cabe."

"No. I'm not."

She was about to breathe a sigh of relief when she paused. Way too easy.

She was right. "I'm ensuring my project assistant has what she needs to be productive and useful at a very important meeting," Cabe said.

Productive and useful! She lifted her chin. "It doesn't take clothes to do that."

Cabe pinched the bridge of his nose and let out a deep sigh. "Why are we arguing about this? You need something to wear. The solution is simple."

"But why do you want to pay for it? I can pur-

chase the outfits myself. You do pay me well."
The second half of her statement was true. As far
as the first part, well, she was on shaky ground
there. She had no idea how expensive this boutique would be. And though she'd rather die than
admit it to Cabe, she had to live on a strict budget and justify the spending of every dime. Or
she'd never have anything left over for a rainy
day after paying off her monthly school loan dues
and taking care of all the other responsibilities.

"That's not the point. The point is, I'm asking you to purchase the items. It's not something
that you have asked for or even want apparently.
Anyway, it's my fault you're unprepared. I should
have warned you about needing some casual
beach clothes."

Irritation flooded through her. Why did he have
to make sense? But his argument did hold some
truth. It wasn't like this was her idea. She would
have no intention of buying more clothes if he
wasn't asking her to.

Cabe obviously saw her softening. He moved

quickly to further rally his point. "It's just another asset."

That was also true. If she needed a different laptop or a new tablet, she wouldn't be expected to pay for it herself.

Besides, she had to admit the utter foolishness of walking into a luxury boutique on her budget and expecting to be able to find something. She doubted a place like that would have a sales rack.

Cabe broke through her thoughts. "If it makes you feel better, consider it a loan."

She worked hard not to grit her teeth. "Oh? How so? Will you be wearing the clothes after I'm done with the meeting?"

His mouth twitched. "An interesting solution. But I was thinking more along the lines of donating the items in the company's name to the women's shelter back in Boston."

That gave her pause. Of course, Cabe immediately sensed her hesitation and pounced.

"You know I'm making sense." He drove the point home.

That may be, Jenna thought, but the fear that

she was tumbling down a dangerous slippery slope sent an icy trickle between her shoulder blades.

He stood staring at her, waiting for her response. She forced herself not to look away from his intense stare. His eyes had grown dark. Due to utter irritation, she'd bet. Cabe probably wasn't used to women turning him down when it came to such offers. Or anything else, for that matter.

The dress would go to good use. It wasn't as if she'd be keeping it. A serpent of doubt crawled into her brain. Was she merely justifying the concept? Giving her head a quick shake, Jenna made herself take a mental step back. She hadn't even seen the dress yet and she was already fretting about having to return it. Cabe continued to stare at her.

She folded her arms across her middle. "Fine. I'll go take a look. If, and only if, I find something that I think may work, then I'll put it on your account. And I will guarantee a donation receipt upon our return from the charity."

"I have no doubt you will."

"Fine."

"Fine," he repeated. "Well, that required more of a battle than it should have. You know, most women would jump at the chance of a shopping spree on the house."

"I am not most women."

He let out an exasperated sigh. "Oh, I'll give you that."

"What is that supposed to mean?" she demanded, ready to do battle yet again for some reason.

He held up his arms in surrender. "I'm agreeing with you. You are definitely not like most of the women I know. Not in the least."

She noticed the slight upward turn of his lips. He was teasing her! And she was falling for it.

She pushed her chair in and stepped away from the desk. "I'm going to take that as a compliment."

He winked at her and her insides quivered like pudding. Not good. Not good at all. A professional, serious Cabe she could handle. She couldn't say the same about this playful one. Or the generous one she'd witnessed on the beach. Or the concerned one who helped put ointment on her bites. Then held her against him as he told her the pressure he'd felt his whole life to be perfect.

Those Cabes were dangerous indeed.

"Go right ahead," he said. "It was meant as one."

As she moved to the door, Jenna had to remind herself that she was irritated.

Cabe reread the same email for the seventh time and found he'd be hard-pressed to recall exactly what it said. He couldn't focus. His mind insisted on wandering to Jenna. No little wonder with her scent still clinging to the air. Things certainly weren't dull when she was around him. This morning alone, she'd managed to have him buy a tableful of island souvenirs and then she'd sparred with him over the simple purchase of a meeting-suitable dress. He hadn't realized how uneventful these trips had been until this time.

This trip had so far been one unexpected adventure after another because of her.

Had she found a dress she liked? Was she trying it on even at this moment?

Those thoughts had him wanting to kick himself. Surely, he had better things to do than contemplate the shopping status of a woman who was merely here to help him with a large venture.

He had to admit, however, that he'd be more than a little disappointed if, after all the back and forth about it, she came back empty-handed. It had not been easy to convince Jenna Townsend to accept something he'd offered to purchase for her. He'd done it twice in one morning.

She would have never accepted if it hadn't been presented as a loan. Pledging the dress to charity had finally trumped it for her. Or so he hoped. He couldn't really be certain of anything when it came to her. Why in the world did he find that so enticing?

He understood. Or thought he did. Jenna had fought fiercely her whole life to become and stay independent. He admired her for it. Who would blame her, growing up as she had? Rather than taking even the slightest risk of becoming like her mother, Jenna had worked hard and sacrificed to make a success of herself. And what a tremendous job she'd done.

His email folder dinged at him again, signaling the arrival of ten more urgent messages in his mailbox. He leaned back in his chair and decided it wasn't even worth his effort to open any of them. His attention was too scattered, a first for him, he admitted with a jolt of surprise. Even more surprisingly, he wasn't going to try to fight it. None of his to-dos were going to get done at this rate anyway. He may as well take a walk over to the shopping center.

Something told him yet another adventure awaited over in that part of the isle.

"Will this be on Mr. Jordan's company account or his personal one?"

Jenna paused at the question.

Cabe had a personal account here? At a women's boutique? The answer dawned on Jenna as she handed her purchases to the impeccably dressed saleslady who'd been helping her.

Cabe had traveled here with other women. Apparently, he had treated them to expensive clothing.

Well, she was not like them. Her situation was completely different. She was here to do a job and work hard to make Cabe's life easier as the CEO of Jordan's Fine Jewelry. Big difference. She did not need to depend on a man to buy her things. She was not like her mother. In fact, the outfit she'd found was quite sensible and quite a bit less costly than many of the other items in the store. Though it was still higher than what she could actually afford herself. But she had managed to find a pair of butter-soft leather sandals that had been drastically marked down. Those were going to be her one and only splurge on this trip as a way to treat herself.

"Definitely the corporate account, please."

The woman began to ring her up and Jenna couldn't help but let her eye travel to the gown sitting on display behind the register. A piece of art—that was the only way to describe it. A shimmery gold color that reminded her of the sand on the beach when the sun hit it just so. Draped over the mannequin like someone had sculptured it into place. The straps holding it up appeared impossibly thin and fragile. She imagined that was an optical illusion. Nothing about this dress appeared to have been left to chance.

She made herself look away. It probably cost more than she made in a year. The saleslady noticed.

"Would you like to try it on?"

Jenna blinked. The thought would have never occurred to her. "Oh, no. That's okay."

"You should. It would look so exotic on someone with your coloring."

Jenna shook her head and took a deep breath. "I'm afraid I'm not in the market for something so glamorous." Especially considering the price would make a nice down payment on a small house.

She smiled. "You're just trying it on. Come, I'd like to see it on you." She moved over to the mannequin and gently began removing the dress. "You'll be doing it for me."

Jenna gave her head a shake. "How so?"

"It will help break up the day and make my shift go a little quicker."

Jenna's heart did a little jump in her chest. Did she dare?

Why not? When would she ever get an opportunity to have an haute couture item actually on her body? She'd probably never even get a chance to set eyes on such a lavish garment again. What could be the harm in indulging in a little fantasy just this once?

And just like that, Jenna found herself in the dressing room, the dress hanging like a golden waterfall off a small garment hook. Her fingers trembled as she handled the silky, delicate material. Light as air and smooth, as though she were somehow holding liquid within her hands. Carefully, she put the gown over her head and gently tugged it down over her shoulders. She closed her eyes as it fell into place.

For several moments, she simply allowed herself to revel in the smooth texture of the material against her skin. Soft and airy, it must have been made from the finest silk.

When she dared a look in the mirror, her breath caught. It was like looking at a different person. A Jenna Townsend she hardly recognized stared back at her. One who belonged in a whole other universe. More magical.

She ran a hand down her midsection and couldn't resist doing a small little spin. The dress twirled around her like a light, airy cloud. Reaching up, she released the complicated clip that held her hair in place and shook out her curls. Giddiness wasn't usually a part of her personality but she felt that way now. She looked good. Better than good. If she had to say so herself, Cinderella had nothing over her in this dress.

She could have been a picture straight out of the pages of an international fashion magazine. Maybe even on the cover. Puckering her lips, she struck a pose in the mirror. Just like those haughty, glamorous runway models. The ones Cabe was always being linked to and seen with.

The idea made her smile. It was silly, she knew, but her heart thudded in her chest at the vision staring back at her from the glass. Who would have thought that a girl from the fringes of South Boston could have pulled off a garment like the one she had on? It was such a far cry from the last formal gown she'd worn. The one she'd scraped and saved for close to a year in order to purchase secondhand for her high school prom. The one she'd stood out like a sore thumb in because it was clearly out of style and clearly used.

If only her former classmates could see her now. Suddenly she wished it with all her heart. Memories of the snickering and sideways glances she'd endured that night came crashing down upon her. No one had said anything, but their knowing, condescending stares communicated it all. She wouldn't let those memories mar this moment.

They wouldn't believe their eyes if they caught a look at her now. She hardly believed her own. Maybe a sneaky invisible little fairy had sprinkled some pixie dust her way and she had entered some kind of delicious alternate universe. And maybe, just maybe, she actually belonged there.

"Are you going to come out so that we may see it?" the saleslady asked from behind the fitting room door, pulling her out of her fanciful thoughts.

"Just one moment." Jenna inhaled deep and straightened to her full length. Such a dress demanded the utmost proper posture. Lifting her chin, she yanked aside the curtain and stepped out of the dressing room then executed a flamboyant, exaggerated bow.

And nearly dropped to the floor when she realized the saleslady hadn't been talking about a figurative "we."

Cabe stood less than three feet away.

CHAPTER SEVEN

CABE FOUND HE could do nothing but stare. He couldn't recall any moment in his life when he'd felt so completely frozen. No words came to his head, no thoughts he could formulate.

His mind zeroed in on one thing and one thing only: Jenna Townsend sheathed in a dress that hugged her so well, all he could do was imagine taking it off her.

She was something out of a portrait. An unearthly goddess who could command an army of men to live or die for her. At the moment, he himself would do anything she bade. The unusual color of the dress matched the golden specks in her hazel eyes. The effect was mesmerizing. He had to remind himself to breathe.

"Cabe." She spoke his name on a whisper. It sounded like a verbal caress beckoning him.

How would it sound if she were to cry it out in pleasure?

His jaw clenched tight. He couldn't think of a thing to say. Here he was, the CEO of a highly successful private company who had to make multimillion-dollar decisions every day. And he'd been struck dumb by a woman in a dress.

She subconsciously ran a hand over her hair. Heaven help him. Her hair. A heavy cascade of dark, flowing curls curtained over her shoulders. He'd feared he'd never see it down. He'd tried to picture the way she would look if she ever saw fit to release it in his presence. But his imagination hadn't nearly done the image justice. Heat raced along his skin. He had to fist his hands at his sides in order to keep from reaching out and running his fingers through the lush, silky strands. His mind may have gone numb but his body knew exactly what it wanted to do.

He swallowed, clenched and unclenched his hands in a strained effort to keep from reaching for her.

She was saying something. He had to force

himself to focus. "…just for fun. I obviously had no intention of trying to buy this."

"A shame." The words came out hoarse, strained even to his own ears.

She narrowed her eyes, and an expression of confusion settled over her features. What didn't she understand? Couldn't she see the effect she was having on him? Not just right at this moment but ever since he'd first laid eyes on her in Boston. He'd never behaved so irrationally. She'd dumped food on him and instead of firing her on the spot he'd promoted her! She teared up watching strangers get married. She attempted to buy a tray full of baubles she didn't need, pretending she wanted every piece. She had an amazing head for business.

And looking at her now took his breath away. *Damn.* This was bad. This was very, very bad. He had lost all control. It was totally unacceptable. He didn't have time for this. His vast experience with women consisted of taking them to a few social gatherings followed by explosive breakups due to his lack of willingness to move things along to the next level. It had suited him just fine. Until now. Now he found himself thinking all sorts of thoughts about the future that he had no business entertaining.

Well, he had to grasp at some kind of sanity. He had too much to do.

Everything in his life was planned out, controlled. That was the only way to avoid regrets and mistakes. He wouldn't allow himself either of those luxuries. He didn't deserve to.

None of his plans included the kind of complications that would result from any kind of fling with a woman like Jenna Townsend.

He knew the best course of action would be to pivot on his heel right now and just hustle right back out of the store.

He couldn't be what she deserved.

Cabe didn't have time for any kind of a real relationship. He had to spend his time and every ounce of his energy proving himself worthy of the Jordan name. What kind of mate or partner would that make him? A lousy one.

The lady standing before him deserved so much more than he could give.

It was settled. He'd made his decision. From now on, he would make sure the relationship between the two of them remained strictly professional. He would keep her at arm's length during the day, and he would make sure to stay off the cursed balcony at night. No more mistakes. He had to promise himself that. He had to guarantee it. All he had to do right now was turn around and leave.

So the next words out of his mouth surprised him indeed. "Come here, Jenna."

Oh, boy.

Jenna took a hesitant step forward. The look on Cabe's face was impossible to read. Was he cross with her? All she'd done was try a dress on. She'd tried to explain she didn't actually intend to buy it.

That idea was preposterous.

He couldn't think she would buy such an extravagant item on the company's account. So what was with the look he currently had on his face? His jaw was tight, his eyes hard, his brows furrowed close together. She couldn't venture a guess what he was thinking. Then again, she'd be hard-pressed to guess what Cabe thought at any given moment.

"I said, come here."

She'd tried to ignore that command, hoping she hadn't heard him right. Her breath caught in her throat, and her limbs didn't seem to want to move. She'd never really seen him angry. Maybe he was about to chew her out and didn't want to do it too loudly. The other woman had made herself scarce. That couldn't be a good sign.

She took a hesitant step forward. "The salesclerk said she wanted to see it on me. I honestly wouldn't even consider actually…"

The words died on her lips as he moved with sudden swiftness, breaching the distance between them. His hand reached out and for one insane moment she thought she might reach for him as well. A bolt of electricity shot through her chest. The room seemed to shrink, to just the small patch of space where the two of them stood.

She felt a rough yet gentle finger trail along her shoulder, up toward her collarbone. There was no way to even try to hide the shudder his touch elicited. Cabe leaned closer, his lips a mere hair's width away from her ear.

She read clear, utter desire on his face.

When he spoke, his breath felt like a subtle caress over the skin on her neck. Her stomach did a flip, the feeling one got when just about to fall but caught herself just in time. Or someone else caught her.

"You need to take this off." Barely a whisper, his command sent a shiver of excitement down her spine.

This couldn't really be happening. She'd obviously fallen down some kind of rabbit hole. Cabe Jordan was not standing in the middle of a chic dress shop with her, telling her to undress.

She swallowed the hard lump that had formed in her throat and licked her suddenly dry lips. "Like I said, it was just in fun."

"Jenna?"

"Yes?"

"We have to go."

"Go?"

Every inch of him was tense, his jaw clenched, his hands fisted at his sides. He looked like he wanted to throw her over his shoulder. The thought had her cheeks burning. She thought of the way he'd almost kissed her and wondered if he would do it again. Heaven help her, she wanted him to. Very much.

"We have to go," he repeated through gritted teeth. "Or we'll be late for our meeting."

If Jenna thought their walk this morning to breakfast had been awkward, their stroll after leaving the shopping center was downright torturous. The fierce blare of the late-afternoon sun didn't help. They passed a lazy-strung hammock slung between palm trees and all Jenna wanted to do was collapse in it for a while. And try not to replay the scene in the dress shop over and over in her head. The way the touch of Cabe's finger had sent a tingling rush over every inch of her skin. She couldn't think about any of that. Instead, she had to somehow focus on a business meeting.

Next to her, Cabe cleared his throat. "That was a smart choice."

She had no idea what he could be referring to. Her brain seemed to have ceased functioning.

"The dress," Cabe added.

What? Was he seriously going to bring it up?

"I mean, you know, the one you have on. Right now. Not that other one." He pointed at her. "This one."

Oh. She could only nod in his direction.

"I don't mean to say that other gown wasn't flattering." He rubbed a hand over his forehead and cursed under his breath.

"It's okay, Cabe. I know what you mean."

He let out a long sigh, his frustration palpable. She fully understood. Life, and this trip, would be so much easier if they had a smooth, uncomplicated relationship. "That makes one of us."

"You're saying this dress I'm wearing now

works well for an important meeting that's being held in a casual, outdoor atmosphere."

"Yes. That's exactly what I'm saying. The light color works well in this heat."

"Thank you."

"You're welcome." He hesitated. "I like your shoes, too," he said after a beat, somewhat wryly.

Jenna glanced down at the strappy, low-heel leather sandals she had on. She'd bought them somewhat impulsively, using her own money, of course. Her navy, thick pumps were not handling well in all this sand. Despite the awkwardness between them, she felt downright giddy that Cabe had noticed.

How schoolgirlish of her.

He suddenly stopped and turned to her. "Jenna, listen—"

Oh, no. No way. He was not going to do this to her. He was not going to try to discuss the dress shop fiasco. Did he want to totally scramble her brain before this meeting?

She didn't break her stride, forcing him to resume walking and catch up.

"So tell me about Sonny," she asked, before he could finish his sentence. Cabe got the hint and followed the change of topic.

Thank heavens for small blessings.

"Sonny is in charge of the retail establishments in the resort's shopping center. He can help us with the latest zoning issue." They turned a corner on the path and Cabe pointed to the distance. "There he is now."

Jenna looked up to see a stout, thick man sitting at a picnic table at a cabana, pounding away at a laptop. Introductions were made when they approached and the three of them wasted no time before getting to the business at hand.

Jenna even managed to focus on taking notes rather than the magnetic pull of the man sitting next to her. No small miracle after this morning and last night.

At the conclusion of the meeting two hours later, she was actually pretty impressed with herself. She'd held her own and even made some useful suggestions.

Now she just had to get through the rest of the day.

After Sonny left, she looked up to find Cabe staring at her. Like a specimen he couldn't understand. She suddenly felt a nervous hitch in the middle of her chest. Perhaps her performance in front of the retail manager hadn't gone as well as she'd thought. Had she done or said something wrong?

"Sonny seems very efficient," she commented, by way of fishing.

"You impressed him." Cabe's answer surprised her. The other man had shown no outward signs of any such thing. In fact, he'd been very matter-of-fact throughout the whole two hours.

"Why do you say that?"

"I've dealt with him quite a bit over the past several months. Trust me, you impressed him."

Jenna swallowed. "I was just trying to get all the details covered."

"You did well."

Her heart thudded at his words. It was one thing to impress Sonny, but to hear Cabe was pleased with her performance sent a lightning bolt of pleasure through her core.

"You're truly one of a kind, Jenna Townsend."

She looked up at him then and realized instantly that this was one of those moments she would never recover from. She was lost—lost in Cabe's steady blue gaze, transfixed by the silky smooth sound of his voice. She'd never find her way again.

She grasped for some kind of response but none would come to her lips. Several seconds went by—she couldn't guess how long. Suddenly, the unmistakable sound of a camera shutter snapped her out of her daze and broke the spell.

"A quick photo, Mr. Jordan." She hadn't even noticed the photographer approach them, holding a large camera to his face and wearing a colorful shirt with the resort logo.

Cabe held his hand up to hold off any further picture taking. "Maybe later." Gently taking Jenna by the elbow, he led her away from the cabana.

Jenna had to remind herself to breathe as they walked away.

"Damn it," Cabe bit out, sparing a glance behind him.

"You don't like your picture taken?"

"Not particularly."

"He's just doing his job."

"Let's hope so," Cabe bit out.

"What do you mean? Isn't he just one of the resort photographers?"

Cabe kept walking, apparently trying to gain as much distance between them and the camera. "Yes, but sometimes my photo doesn't merely end up in a souvenir frame for me to purchase."

"Where does it end up?"

"Too often it ends up in a tabloid or some tawdry website."

It took a moment but his meaning slowly dawned on her. He wasn't merely upset that his picture had been taken. Cabe was upset that it had been taken *with her.*

"Will Carmen be cross with you?" she blurted out without thinking.

Cabe paused then, just long enough to give her a confused look. "Carmen? No. I mean, I guess not. I honestly don't know."

She merely nodded as they resumed walking. "You're not worried about her potential reaction to the photo, then?"

"The thought hadn't even crossed my mind."

That was interesting. Then again, Carmen was probably one of those women so secure with her beauty and attractiveness she probably wouldn't have cared if Cabe had taken a hundred pictures with someone like her. The likes of Jenna Townsend were certainly not enough to elicit any kind of jealous reaction from an international supermodel.

"I thought maybe that's why you wanted to avoid the camera."

His answer was notably matter-of-fact. "Carmen and I broke up. Just before I left Boston."

Jenna nearly stumbled before she recovered her step. She had no business feeling giddy at that bit of news. "I'm sorry to hear that."

Cabe shrugged. "Don't be. It was bound to happen."

"I see."

"Carmen's been pursuing a movie career for as long as I've known her. She finally got her big break this past month. She'll be filming a horror piece. In the Amazon. She asked me to visit her. I said I didn't have that kind of time."

"Oh." Jenna took a deep breath. If Cabe was shaken over the breakup, he certainly had shown no signs of heartbreak. Not that she'd ever expect a man like Cabe Jordan to wear his heart on his sleeve when it came to women. Still, Jenna didn't detect any sense of loss or regret. Well, she had no business speculating on that. Or hoping the notion to be true. "Then, if you don't mind my asking…"

Cabe finally stopped, took her by the arm and gently turned her to face him. "Spit it out, Jenna."

"Why are you so agitated about the photographer, then?"

She knew she shouldn't have asked. And wanted to kick herself when he answered.

"I really don't want a picture of the two of us plastered all over the gossip sites."

Jenna felt the lump form in her throat and made herself swallow it down. She understood, she really did. She knew whatever was happening between them right now on this resort wasn't reality. Once they were back in the States, they would go back to living their regular lives. She'd return to her boring, repetitive existence back in Boston. And Cabe would return to his exciting life in Manhattan. Why would he want to answer anyone's questions about public photos with his project manager?

He took a different way through the center of the island in order to ensure they'd ditched the photographer. And besides, this route held something Cabe wanted Jenna to see.

He had to catch her as she stepped on the wooden hanging bridge. Or else Jenna was headed for a dramatic face-plant. Cabe didn't realize how fast he'd been walking or how Jenna had made sure to keep up with him. Unfortunately, she'd miscalculated the steadiness of the wobbly bridge and was about to fall over. "Here. I've got you," Cabe said, taking her by the arm and gently pulling her up.

She gave him a look of surprise and gratitude, and then her gaze fell to the hand that held her arm. Her skin felt smooth and warm under his touch.

She gently pulled her arm free and took hold of the thick rope railing.

"Thanks. Guess I'm still breaking into these new sandals."

"You can always take them off. Feel free to go barefoot, now that our business day is over."

She gave him a small smile that didn't really reach her eyes. "Can we slow down now? I think we lost our tail."

"Sorry. I didn't realize how fast I was walking. Not like the photographer was actually following us."

"Well, we couldn't have risked that now, could we?" Her voice held a hint of annoyance.

He didn't want to be the reason Jenna's picture was pasted all over the internet. He'd grown used to the lack of privacy over the years. But for someone as inexperienced with it as Jenna was, the intrusion could be daunting and upsetting. She'd done nothing to deserve that. Not to mention what his parents would say.

"Like I said, I'd rather not give the tabloids any fodder."

"Got it," Jenna replied. "I am clearly not an ideal photo op."

Her tone was sharp. "Something wrong?" he asked.

She let out a deep sigh. "No. Nothing at all."

He waited a beat but she didn't go on. "Doesn't sound like it's nothing. Is there something you'd like to say?"

Her cheeks suddenly turned pink with annoyance. Maybe even anger.

Which made no sense. All he'd done was try to spare her the unwanted scrutiny an international photograph would garner. But Jenna remained frustratingly silent.

"You have no idea what kind of attention one

lousy picture can elicit," he told her. "I was trying to protect you."

She blinked and her expression softened. "Is that the only reason? That was all for me?"

What in the devil's name was she talking about? Of course it was. "You are clearly a very private person, Jenna. I didn't think you'd appreciate such an intrusion."

He waited as she let that sink in.

"I guess you're right," she said, looking up and finally noticing their surroundings. They had reached the majestic waterfalls at the center of the resort. Surrounded by lush greenery and gray rocks, three high waterfalls dropped close to a hundred feet into a crystal-blue river. A series of rustic wooden bridges like the one they currently stood on webbed throughout the area.

Jenna's expression held wonder and awe, as he knew it would. Their swift jaunt just now had brought a rosy hue to her cheeks, and her lips remained parted. "Wow, this is beautiful."

Breathtaking, Cabe thought. But he wasn't thinking of the scenery. Jenna's skin glistened

with the thin sheen of mist that drifted in the air.
She looked like a heavenly angel ascended from
paradise.

"Why did it bother you so much, Jenna? That I
had us run from the photographer?" he prompted.
The situation had triggered something in her,
something he wanted to get to the bottom of.
This was a perfect spot to do it.

Her eyes narrowed on his face. "You were saying how clearly guarded I am."

"Yes?"

She blew out a deep breath, went back to studying the scenery. "I didn't exactly have an ideal
upbringing, Cabe. As you very well know."

"I know you didn't have it easy. And I know
how much you've overcome to get to where you
are."

She sniffed. "I'm Amanda Townsend's daughter. The town drunk, the desperate single mom
who flirted with everyone's husband."

"None of that was your fault, Jenna."

"I know. But it was certainly my responsibility.
It fell on me to take care of her when she drank

so much she was sick for days. It fell on me to find a way to feed and care for my brother when there was no food or money to be found."

He ached to hold her, to erase her past and pain somehow. She deserved so much better than what she'd been handed in life. Unlike himself. "You were the caregiver, even though your brother was older."

She smiled, with genuine affection clear on her face. "We split responsibilities. He's protected me in myriad ways, too, over the years. A girl tends to get picked on when she's known as the trashy daughter of the town's trashy drunk."

"You and Sam are lucky to have each other."

He heard her inhale deeply, slowly let the breath out. He'd do anything to bear some of the weight on her shoulders, if only he could.

"I suppose we are. I can't imagine dealing with Amanda over the years without him. Though sometimes I wish he didn't have to deal with it at all. That I was a single child, for his sake." A small laugh escaped her lips. "I used to daydream that someone rich would show up one day and adopt—" She stopped suddenly and cupped her hand over her mouth, as if she could pull back the half-spoken word that hung in the air.

"It's not all it's cracked up to be," he said.

"I'm so sorry," Jenna whispered. "I should have known better than to say something like that."

"It's okay, Jenna. It's a common fantasy among children. Funny thing is, I had the opposite daydream."

"What do you mean?"

"After I found out, I kept having these visions of my real parents appearing at the door one day. To tell me how sorry they were that they ever gave me up. Then they would beg me to forgive them, ask if they could take me back." He grew somber as the memory further surfaced. "Then I would feel terrible. Guilty for hoping to leave James and Tricia when they were so sad." What a silly kid he'd been. Worrying himself sick over a fantasy that had no basis in reality.

"You've been trying to prove yourself for as long as you can remember, haven't you?" she asked in a soft voice.

"I guess I have. It's hard to live up to a ghost."

"A ghost?"

"James and Tricia adopted me after losing their biological son. Unlike you, I may not have had an actual living, breathing sibling. But his presence was always there. Right down to the room my parents never altered after he died." A room he was never allowed to so much as enter.

"They never emptied his room?" Jenna asked, her voice breaking.

"No, never."

"Cabe, there was no way you could have reached them. Nothing you could have done. They were broken and shattered over their loss."

"It's tough for a child to see through all that."

She leaned closer. "You never stopped trying, did you? To make them happy?" She was close enough that he could read her eyes even in the dim light. They held no pity. If anything, she appeared to be looking at him with something resembling admiration. "Cabe, you deserve to be happy."

Her words hammered into his soul. In one simple sentence she'd cut to the very core of him, through to all his childhood insecurities and disappointments.

"Jenna, you amaze me," he told her. He'd never made a truer statement. He thought back to that first day in Boston. It horrified him how insensitive he'd been. He should have realized someone like Jenna, who'd had a lifetime of trying to escape the shadow of her mother's reputation, would take questions about the theft personally.

And just now, with the photographer. She'd thought he was ashamed to be seen with her for the very same reason. Jenna's whole life had been about others judging her based on the actions of her mother. He could be such a careless, thoughtless lout at times.

"This conversation is getting pretty deep," Jenna said quietly in a tone that broke his heart. "Too deep to be having with my boss." She let out a small laugh, clearly forced.

If only she could really see him, not just as a boss, but as a man. A man who wanted to unearth the many layers that were Jenna Townsend.

"Do me a favor," Cabe began. "Take a good look around this place. A really good look."

She did as he asked, although not before giving him a confused frown. "It's wondrous. I didn't realize places like this actually existed." Jenna ducked her head shyly, as if embarrassed by what she'd just revealed.

"It's all an illusion."

"What do you mean?"

"That large waterfall in the middle, that was in the original landscape. The other two smaller ones on either side, those were formed by manipulating the cliff side. Just like everything else in this place, it's been painstakingly planned and created. None of it is genuine or the real thing. Just like me," he added, meeting her eyes.

The lines on her forehead deepened. "Cabe, why would you think that?" Maybe she did see the real him after all.

Before he could answer, a strong gust of wind shook the bridge they stood on. Without giving it a thought, Cabe reached to grab her around her middle and pulled her closer, both feeling and hearing her sharp intake of breath. "Sorry, these bridges aren't really meant to stand around on for extended periods of time." He spoke low against her ear.

"Right. They're more for appearances as well."

"It would seem." It was safe to let go now, but he continued to hold her anyway. For some reason, he couldn't seem to stop touching Jenna. He would enjoy it while he could. For now, he was simply happy that she made no attempt to step out of his embrace.

"Why was it me?" he blurted out. Her eyes searched his even as her touch soothed him, comforted him. So he went on. "I wonder about it every day. The mere randomness of it."

"Oh, Cabe." She reached for him then and he felt as if time had stopped. Her soft, delicate fingers found his face then ran gently along his jaw. He reflexively dipped his head into her touch.

"I'm also a made product, Jenna. As artificial and fake as these waterfalls. I'm not an original. I'm not any kind of rarity. I was merely randomly selected, treated and polished to transform into someone else entirely. A lie. A falsehood I've lived every day of my life. It's hard not to feel like a fraud. My parents lost their real son. Their one and only precious child. And somehow I was chosen by some mysterious twist of fate to step in and take the life he was meant to lead."

To his shock, she stepped farther into his embrace. A shiver ran through him at her closeness. He knew one of them should pull away. But, heaven help him, it wasn't going to be him.

Her eyes glistened and it tore at his heart. She remained silent, giving him time to continue if he desired. Apparently, he did. "I have everything. And he's gone. How can my mother and father not resent me for that? They tried so hard not to show it. But I could tell by their indifference. I could see. How in the world would I blame them?"

"You worked hard for all that you have, Cabe," she said. "Everyone knows how much you've done for Jordan's Fine Jewelry. The way it grew once you took over."

"Maybe so. But so much of it was handed to me."

She gave her head a small shake. "You aren't giving yourself any credit. I can't even imagine the company being run by anyone else. You're really good."

"I had to be good." He tightened his grip around her waist, pulled her closer. And she felt so right up against him. "Don't you see?"

"See what?"

"The reality is, I can't squander it. It has to mean something that it was me." He took a deep breath, inhaled the scent of her shampoo. "After all, I'm the Jordan Golden Boy."

She shook her head slowly. "I know who you are. You're Cabe Jordan. A talented and accomplished CEO. You've done so much for your employees. And you're a credit to your parents. Just today you changed the life of a young girl you just happened to see selling cheap jewelry on the beach. You're the kind of man any woman with a pulse would fall head over heels—"

The roaring in his ears kept him from hearing any more. He didn't need to. What he needed was to taste her, to feel her up against him. Inside his very soul. Pulling her even closer, he took her mouth and plunged in. She tasted like heaven, like redemption, like everything he could have hoped for.

He'd never be able to let her go.

This was a fairy tale. She was convinced now. Or it was a sweet, unimaginable dream. Jenna hoped never to wake up. Cabe held her tight against him, his mouth devouring hers. She wrapped her arms around his neck and shifted her hips closer against his, felt the strength of his desire for her. The knowledge made her skin burn. This dazzling, enigmatic man wanted her. She'd seen the longing on his face, and now could feel it in the power of his kiss and in the reaction of his body.

"Jenna," he whispered against her mouth, his voice full of longing. A heady shiver of need ran up her spine. "Tell me. I have to know."

She couldn't think, couldn't seem to breathe. What was he asking for? She'd give him anything. Her soul, her heart. Anything. So she simply answered yes.

His hands moved down her rib cage, down farther along her hips. Then she felt herself suddenly hoisted off the ground. He lifted her completely off her feet and started to carry her, steady and balanced despite the crooked and wobbly bridge. She couldn't tear her gaze off Cabe's face. His eyes reminded her of the ocean during a violent storm—dark and shadowed. The sound of the crashing water grew fainter and fainter behind them. She couldn't guess where they were going, but would let him take her anywhere. As long as he never stopped holding her.

She wanted so much more. She wanted all of him.

She'd wanted him since the moment he walked into her office. No, she'd wanted him since she'd known him, practically her whole life.

Cabe was the star of her daydreams, her girlhood crush. He'd transformed her life since walking back into it. He'd transformed *her*. She didn't recognize this reckless, careless woman she'd become. Was she really kissing her boss outside in the open, where anyone could walk by? This wasn't like her—this was downright wanton. But she didn't care. All she cared about was having Cabe completely.

He carried her out of the maze of bridges. The sounds of the waterfalls echoed soothingly behind them. An unseen bird chirped a melody in one of the trees above. He clearly knew the island well. The path he took her on was completely deserted. Before she realized, they were somehow in the hallway outside his suite. Cabe managed to unlock the door and bring her into his room, still holding her tight in his embrace. Slowly, he set her down on the thick, plush comforter on the bed.

She was in Cabe Jordan's hotel room as he kissed her and caressed her. The ocean view outside the balcony window looked like a painting created by a master painter. Her desire-fogged mind told her this all had to be some separate fantasy away from the rest of the universe.

And she would pretend it was. She would make believe she was in a universe where Jenna Townsend for once in her life got what she wanted. One where she succumbed to her desires. Just this one time, with this one man. Gently, slowly, he lowered himself to balance on his elbows just above her.

"Jenna?" He said her name as a question, touchingly making sure this was what she wanted.

It was, more than anything. She answered him by slowly undoing the top of her dress. She didn't get a chance to unbutton the rest. Covering her mouth with his once again, Cabe took over, making quick work of the remaining buttons.

There was no doubt in her mind. She wanted him. It was the only thing that mattered in this moment. Jenna knew this was what paradise would feel like.

Cabe confirmed it by taking her straight there.

She'd fallen asleep in his arms.

Cabe ran his fingers through Jenna's soft, thick hair. He sat cradling her with her back against his chest. Outside his window, the ocean shone like a rare glittering jewel in the distance.

Let her sleep, he thought. This moment would

be over all too soon. Once they stepped out of this room, reality would set in. Then he would have to examine what had just happened. But not now.

Now he was just going to enjoy the feel of Jenna's languid body against his, savor the sensation of what it had felt like to hold her and love her.

He stroked her hair, breathed in the scent of her tropical shampoo mingled with the salty sea air. Jenna was not like anyone he'd ever known. That she was still helping her mother, even as an adult, didn't surprise him. This amazing, dynamic woman in his arms was the type of person who'd never turn away from anyone who needed her. Didn't she realize how special that made her?

Thinking of what she must have endured as a child made him want to throw something. Or punch the headrest behind him. She really was extraordinary. Jenna had prospered and shone into adulthood despite the genetic cards she'd been dealt. She'd worked hard and earned it all. Unlike those who'd had everything handed to them. Unlike him.

Suddenly, he felt lacking, inadequate. Jenna had accomplished so much in her life despite being given so little. Compared to her struggles, he'd had it so easy. All he had to do was take advantage of all the ample opportunities he'd been awarded.

The memory of the first day of his Boston visit flashed through his mind's eye. Her anger had been vibrant and strong. He'd deserved her ire then. He'd been an utter ass. When he thought about what that must have felt like for her, to have the boss come to town and practically accuse her of being a thief.

He was her boss, the CEO. Someone who had a direct say on her career, her very future.

And he'd just made love to her.

A bubble of acid churned in his gut. Damn his impulsiveness.

Jenna wasn't the type to have a meaningless office fling. She had substance, character. With all that she'd been through, she had every right to a bright and fulfilling future. Complete with the rewarding career and a caring steady man who would always be there for the woman in his life.

She deserved the kind of future Cabe would never be able to give her.

For one hazy moment upon awakening, Jenna thought perhaps she had dreamed it all. There wasn't any kind of way the fates would have really allowed it to happen. She had *not* just been intimate with Cabe Jordan.

"Hey there, Sleeping Beauty." His rich baritone served to pull her out of that fallacy very quick. As did the weightlessness in her muscles. Not to mention the warm body she was snuggled against.

Dear heavens. What had she done? How could she have just made love with her *boss*?

Scrambling to gain some sense, she removed herself out of his embrace and stood up off the bed with the top sheet wrapped around her. Cabe sat up at the edge of the mattress and rammed a hand through his hair.

A glance at the window showed the sky had

turned a deep, rich purple. The hour had to be approaching early evening. They'd apparently been there awhile. What time was it? She never wore a watch but where was her phone? She had no idea. If she had dropped it on the bridge, she hadn't even done a backup since arriving.

How utterly unprofessional—she didn't even know where her phone was. But then again, so was sleeping with someone she worked with. Correct that—Cabe was the man she worked *for*. The blood left her brain. She dared a glance in his direction. He was clearly avoiding looking at her.

Cabe cleared his throat. "We should probably go get cleaned up."

"Um, I seem to have misplaced my phone." Great. On top of everything else, she had to admit to misplacing company property.

They both saw it at the same time, resting on the carpet near the leg of the bed. Disastrously, they both bent to reach for it, bumping heads.

This had to be the most awkward moment of her life. She had no idea how to process it. There were no excuses but she'd just felt so off balance on the bridge by the waterfall, literally and figuratively. Cabe's anguished face coupled with the way he'd opened up to her. And the location. It was all a perfect storm of overstimulation and she'd just snapped. She'd given in to her aching desire to be close to him. In every way.

Straightening, she took a deep breath. "Cabe, I—"

He held a hand up to stop her. "Let's just both get cleaned up. I, for one, could use a long hot shower before dressing for dinner."

Jenna winced. He'd effectively just dismissed her. There had to be a large sinkhole or underground cave on this island she could go crawl in. Or better yet, she could run into the ocean and dive into a large wave, just swim out into the open sea. It couldn't be any worse. She already felt like she was drowning.

"Probably a good idea." She forced out her agreement and grabbed her phone off the floor.

And her blood went cold again. Her screen was lit up with text messages. Most of them from home. Her mother. She could think of no good reason for Amanda to be trying to reach her here. The messages could only mean one thing: Amanda was in some kind of trouble.

CHAPTER EIGHT

CABE JORDAN HAD made love to her—there was no way to focus on anything else.

Jenna lathered up the rich mango gel soap and let the soothing water of the shower wash over her still-tingling skin.

She could still feel his touch. Every word he'd whispered in her ear still echoed in her head. Every second of what they'd shared would be ingrained in her memory for the rest of her life. She'd never forget the way he'd felt, the things he'd said to her. It would all torture her for the rest of her life. Stifling a sob, Jenna turned off the water and grabbed the thick Turkish robe hanging from the shower door, wrapping it around herself and stepping out of the stall. Cabe had said he would wait for her in his room while she got cleaned up. She had no idea what she would say to him. He couldn't possibly know how torn she felt right now.

How in the world could she have let things get so far between them? And what in heaven's name was she to do now?

The beeping of her cell phone interrupted her thoughts again. Two more texts came in, and several missed calls registered.

Not now…not just yet.

She just couldn't tackle any of it now, not on top of everything else she had to grapple with. Call her a coward, but despite knowing that she should just answer the phone and find out what was happening back in Boston, her nerves just couldn't handle anything else at the moment. First she had to gain back some of her equilibrium before she faced Cabe. She would deal with Amanda's newest crisis when she regained some semblance of sanity and strength. A couple of hours more when she was half a world away certainly couldn't make any sort of difference anyway.

With shaky hands, Jenna gripped the phone

and pressed the reset button until her finger hurt. When the device finally powered off, she sank down onto the love seat against the wall of her room. Her knees had suddenly gone weak.

What a fool she'd been. Forgetting about her reality for even a few moments of guilty pleasure. Pretending she could escape who she truly was. Her truth had even found her here, on this beautiful island paradise.

She could never be anything to someone like Cabe Jordan.

She had too much baggage, too much of a responsibility, the likes of which he'd never be able to relate to. An alcoholic mother who was repeatedly in and out of jail. Dear God, Amanda may even need bailing out right at this very moment. Or perhaps she'd been evicted again and couldn't get ahold of Jenna's brother nor find the spare key to her apartment that Jenna had given her.

Cabe was worried about a reporter simply posting a picture of the two of them. She shuddered to think how he would feel about being tied to a woman whose mother had such a sordid past.

The press would have a field day with Amanda's history.

Well, there was nothing Jenna could do about it now, being hundreds of miles away on a Caribbean island.

Jenna took a deep breath and forced herself up. First thing first, Cabe awaited her. She had to shake off the self-pity and get dressed. They planned to get an early dinner at a seaside tavern and then head over to the casino. As far as she knew, none of those plans had changed.

How was she going to face him? Just a couple of short hours ago they'd been as close and as intimate as any two people could be. But next time she faced him, things had to be different. She had no one but herself to blame. She'd let her guard down, let herself forget who she was and where she belonged on the hierarchy of life.

Somehow, she had to rectify all that. What had happened between them this afternoon could never happen again. She had to make sure of it, even though it was breaking her heart into a million jagged pieces.

Pieces that would never be put back together no matter how hard she tried.

Jenna refused to meet him in the eye.

For the life of him, Cabe couldn't figure out what to say to break the ice. Should he apologize? Or would that just make things even more awkward? One thing was certain—the silence was becoming unbearable.

He cleared his throat, decided to go with something mundane, just to start. "I hope you're hungry. This place has quite an extensive buffet. Everything from seafood to the finest Kobe steak."

Again, she didn't face him, barely turned her head. "Sounds good."

Cabe stifled a groan of irritation. He deserved this; he'd done it to himself. Jenna clearly wanted to take back what had happened between them. He could guess why. They were completely wrong for each other. He'd never be able to give her the kind of things she deserved from a man.

Jenna needed someone with substance, a man

who could give her a future. She'd grown up with enough instability. She didn't need any in her adulthood.

Between his nonstop workdays and his life-style, Cabe couldn't pretend to be that man. Hell, he barely stayed in the same city for more than two weeks at a time. She was smart enough to see that. A future with him wouldn't be much of a future at all. Not for someone who had as much going for her as Jenna did.

He should never have touched her, never so much as let himself stroke a hair on her head.

He had no excuse, only the fact that once again he'd proved what a weak person he was. His re-sistance had completely crumbled when she'd cupped his face and uttered soothing words no one had ever said to him before, her voice full of concern.

He would have to find a way to apologize. If not with words, then with some kind of way that would make all this up to her.

The soft music of a steel-drum band started up behind them on the beach as the maître d' greeted them. It took all of Cabe's will not to touch her as they were being led to their table. He wanted so badly to place his hand at the small of her back, feel the heat of her skin beneath his touch.

He cursed under his breath. To anyone in the dining area, they appeared to be the perfect picture of a well-suited couple enjoying each other's company while on vacation.

He would never have that. Not with Jenna. Not with anyone. How silly of him to believe that even for a moment he could. He'd long lost his appetite. Jenna hardly looked interested in food either. But it appeared they were both willing to go through the pretense.

But she surprised him when the waiter appeared. Instead of her usual water or iced tea, she asked for a glass of wine. He lifted an eyebrow in question after the man had left. "Looking for something a bit stronger this evening?"

She ducked her head when answering. "I'm afraid there isn't anything strong enough."

Cabe indulged in a deep sigh. Enough was enough. "Jenna, I think it's time we faced this head-on. Something happened between us. Something major."

She ducked her head. "I know that."

Unable to help himself, he reached for her hand across the table. At her flinch, he hastily pulled it back.

He just didn't learn, did he? Always taking too much, offering too little in return.

The tension between them hung thick and palpable.

"Maybe we should just cancel the visit to the casino," Cabe suggested, pulling his hand back. In an act of self-preservation, Jenna had jumped when he'd reached for her. As much as she might long for it, she lost all her resolve when he touched her. "I don't think either of us is really in the right frame of mind," he added. "Maxim will have to understand."

Great. Another work obligation that was being impacted because of her. She shook her head. "It's okay. That won't be necessary."

Try as she might, Cabe saw through her attempt to act professional. He rammed his fingers through his hair. "Jenna, please. Just say something. Tell me what's going on in your head."

Her eyes stung. There was really no good way to begin. "Oh, Cabe. We both know there's really only one thing to say."

He lifted an eyebrow. "And that is?"

"It's all wrong, what's happened between us."

He sucked in a breath, looked away. "Trust me when I say I didn't see it coming, either, the way I suddenly feel about you."

She shook her head, held her hands up. The lump in her throat made it hard to speak but she pushed through it. "That's what I mean. You can't do that."

"Do what?"

"I can't hear about how you feel about me. Nor think about how I feel about you. I can't do this, any of this. This project is too important to me. My job is too important. I can't believe I jeopardized everything by sleeping with my boss." A deep shudder shook her through her core. Her heart felt like it was splitting down the middle. And there was nothing she could do.

"Who says you jeopardized anything?"

"It's the truth. My reputation means everything to me."

"And it's still intact."

She shook her head. "Maybe for now. But everything I've worked for, none of it will matter if people find out I was intimate with the boss on a business trip!"

"It's not as scandalous as it sounds."

How she wished he was right, that things could be different between them. That she could somehow actually be sitting here and enjoying a moonlit dinner by the ocean with the man she— She gave her head a shake. That word kept popping up. And she had to stop even thinking it. Imagine, she'd practically said it out loud to Cabe at the waterfall earlier. What did it matter if she knew she was in love with him, that perhaps she'd always been in love with him? The cold slap of reality was all that mattered now.

"Jenna, I never meant to put you in such a position. It just kind of happened. I'm not sure what I can do to make it up to you, but I promise you I will. I'll think of some way."

The blood left her brain. "Oh, my God. You're not suggesting that I get some kind of reward because of what happened between us! Like some kind of—"

He jolted in his seat. "No! Of course not. I just mean— I don't know what I meant. Just that I hate what's happening, what you're feeling right now."

Suddenly it was too much. The events of the afternoon, the mystery texts and phone calls. This whole conversation. She just had to get away. Without a thought as to how it would look, she rose from her seat and dropped her napkin onto the table. "Excuse me."

Cabe stood as well. "Jenna, wait."

She didn't. The waiter gave them both a curious look but Jenna didn't care. She needed to get away. Cabe was fast on her heels. Part of her wished he would stop chasing her. But another foolish part would be crushed if he let her just run off into the night.

He kept on. She heard him calling her name behind her, felt a sharp pang of guilt for ignoring him. But she couldn't bring herself to stop, couldn't let Cabe see the tears in her eyes, the anguish that had to be written all over her face.

Her nerves couldn't handle the conversation that would ensue if he caught up to her. She'd fallen for him. Cabe was a known playboy who had a new woman on his arm more often than the moon changed phases. She knew she could never be anything more than a flippant affair for him. And yet she'd still gone and risked her professional career.

For a few moments of pleasure, she'd risked everything.

She figured it would just be a matter of time before he found her, and she was right. When he did, she was sitting on a large boulder on the edge of the beach, her toes submerged in the sand. She didn't look up at him as he approached.

"Hey there," he ventured.

"Hey."

"Mind if I sit?"

She didn't respond but shifted slightly to make room for him on the big rock. And instantly regretted it. Hardly a hair separated them, and his warmth seeped through her skin. And brought back unwanted memories of this afternoon, the absolute last thing she needed to be thinking about.

"I keep saying the wrong thing to you," he told her, looking straight ahead. She'd inadvertently run toward the casino. They could see its bright and colorful lights in the distance across the water.

"It's not you," she answered.

He grunted. "I beg to differ."

"We both seem to be stumbling here." She was just so embarrassed. And downright disappointed in herself.

"So…maybe we just move forward, acknowledge that even the best of us make mistakes?"

The word made her cringe, but he was right. "I guess we don't have much choice."

They sat in awkward silence, for how long Jenna couldn't guess. Cabe's sigh finally broke through it. "Well. There it is. That's the grand Paraiso Casino," he said, nodding his head in its direction.

She followed his gaze across the water. Even from this distance she could tell she had no business there. The place was completely out of her league. A steady stream of sports cars and luxury sedans pulled up the circular driveway. Those cars cost more than she'd hope to make in several years. Much more.

The people emerging out of those cars looked elegant and regal. Men in tuxedos and women in gowns. She looked down at her simple outfit. She'd been resourceful, finding a fitted black blouse in the boutique this afternoon to match one of her slim business suit skirts. At the time, she'd felt great pride for coming up with the idea and making it work. Now she felt like a lowly pauper who'd thought she could sneak into the prince's ball.

Which was exactly who she was.

"I've never been to a casino before," she admitted.

"Really? There are quite a few in New England. You haven't even been to any of those?"

She shrugged. "I'm not much of a gambler."

"Well, if you'd like, I could show you how to play some of the tables."

"No, thanks. Gambling's not really a habit I want to pick up." She wouldn't bother to explain that her aversion to gambling was due to another one of her mother's failings. How many times had Amanda skirted her parental duties to go spend time on the slots? How many times had she gambled away money they could have desperately used for food or rent?

"I understand," Cabe told her. And somehow, she knew he did, that he grasped exactly what she was referring to. That was part of the problem. She felt as if Cabe understood her better than anyone else ever had. It was one of the reasons she'd forsaken all sanity earlier and let herself become intimate with him.

"Well, you get to tour one right now," he said and clapped his hands in mock excitement. "I guess I better get you over there before Maxim sends out a search party for us. We're already late."

Great. So now she could add tardiness to her list of professional missteps on this trip. She suppressed a groan of irony. In the overall scheme of things, being late to meet her casino tour guide was relatively trivial.

"We'll be taking a boat there," Cabe added.

"A boat?"

He nodded in the building's direction. "The casino is on its own little island, across the water. I'll drop you off."

"You won't be joining us?"

He shrugged. "He only mentioned you specifically."

"He did?"

"Uh-huh. And I guess you shouldn't keep him waiting."

She should be relieved, Jenna thought. But instead a dull disappointment settled in her chest. She didn't want to spend the evening with Maxim. She wanted to spend it with the man right next to her. Laughing with him, enjoying the warm tropical air. But this was for the best. It would give her some time to sort out her thoughts, settle her nerves. Things she had no hope of doing with Cabe anywhere nearby. It made sense. So why did she want to cry? To beg him to stay by her side? She bit her lip to stop herself from doing so.

They made it to a dock where a small open-air boat waited. A smiling captain took her hand and helped her on board. It appeared no other passengers were embarking for this go-around.

At her quizzical look Cabe responded, "All the avid gamblers are already at the tables. We're a little late to the party."

Only it wasn't going to be a party at all. Not if Cabe wasn't going to be there with her. The boat revved up and started a steady path across the water. The breeze suddenly picked up and made her shiver. Without a word, Cabe slipped off his suit jacket and draped it over her shoulders. The warmth of his body against the fabric cocooned her skin. She resisted the urge to snuggle deeply into it. "Thank you."

"It can get chilly on the water. I should have warned you."

Her heart ached as she thought of the picture they must have made. Alone on a boat on their way to a glamorous casino, his jacket draped over her shoulders to keep her warm. She wanted so much to make believe the idyllic picture could be reality.

But how could it given who she was and where she came from? How soon would someone like Cabe start noticing similarities between herself and the woman who at this very moment was still texting her? Because that needy woman would always text. Amanda would never be out of her life. And Cabe didn't need that kind of lowbrow drama in his.

Jenna knew better. Some things were simply not meant to be.

* * *

Maxim stood waiting for them as they disembarked. He greeted her with a warm smile and a barely-there nod to Cabe. Cabe offered a small grunt in response. Any other time, she might have found the competitive aura between the two men humorous and maybe even flattering. But not right now. She had too much on her mind. Too much to deal with. Her pocketbook buzzed yet again with another message on her phone.

Maxim stood staring at her. Cabe looked at her expectantly. One of them had obviously just asked her a question.

Jenna forced a smile and nodded, hoping it was an adequate response to whatever may have just been posed to her. Cabe's eyes grew wide. And clouded with something else she couldn't name. Hurt? By contrast, Maxim's grin had grown two-fold. Oh, dear, what had she just agreed to?

"I guess I'll leave you two to yourselves, then," Cabe said then turned away. Her heart plummeted. Apparently, she'd just agreed to being alone with Maxim, essentially sending Cabe

away. The exact opposite of what she really
wanted. For one insane moment, Jenna wanted
to yell at him to stop, to run after him and just
explain everything. That she was oh, so wrong
for him. That she had too much baggage. She'd
never be the type of woman Cabe Jordan needed
to have on his arm at his swanky social func-
tions and his family gatherings. She wanted to
tell him all that. And then beg him to want her
anyway.

But Maxim was speaking to her. She'd better
listen this time. Who knew what she would agree
to next without meaning to? Besides, Cabe had
already walked several feet away. How foolish
would it look to chase after him like a silly twit?

"Let's go find you a drink, my dear," Maxim
offered. "Then we'll get the tour started." Dear
heavens. The last thing she needed tonight was
another drink.

What she needed, down to her soul, was to
have Cabe back by her side. He was her anchor, a
tether in this alien world full of riches and excess.
Maxim was nice enough, every inch the atten-

tive gentleman. Any single woman with a pulse would be thrilled to have him as her very own personal guide for the evening. Just not Jenna.

To top it off, she might have just hurt Cabe. She'd certainly be hurt if he'd dismissed her the same way. To spend time with another man, no less. Professional or not.

Meanwhile, her phone kept buzzing, buzzing, buzzing... Jenna cursed Amanda under her breath. She'd been cursing her all night. What did her mother want? Maybe ignoring her hadn't been the wisest decision, because now she could hardly think of anything else. What fresh hell had Amanda created for them all this time?

They'd made it to the entrance of the grand casino when Maxim turned to her. "Are you all right, dear?" he asked, concern etched in his face. "You look a little pale."

Jenna gave her head a shake and placed her hand on her midsection. "I'm afraid something I've eaten doesn't seem to be agreeing with me." It wasn't exactly a lie. "I'm not used to such rich food, as delicious as everything is."

Maxim gave her a sympathetic nod and pointed behind her. "The ladies' restroom is down that hallway. Take your time."

She gave him a grateful smile and turned on her heel. When she got there, the restroom was blessedly empty. Taking a breath to steady her nerves, she fished her phone out of her small purse. Without giving herself a chance to change her mind, she pulled up her brother's contact file and clicked on it.

It was time to face the piper. And the harsh reality that was her life.

He answered on the first ring. "Hey, sis."

"Sam, what's going on back in Boston? Amanda's calling and texting me relentlessly."

Sam sighed deeply before he spoke. "It's bad, Jen. You should probably sit down."

Oh, no. Jenna leaned back against the tiled wall. "Just tell me."

By the time he finished, Jenna really was going to be sick. According to Sam, the person who'd robbed Jordan's Fine Jewelry, committing the

crime that had started Jenna on this whole jour-
ney, had been discovered.

That person was her mother.

She'd barely said three words to him last night
as he walked her back to her hotel room. Cabe
shuffled the papers on the table in the conference room and glanced at the door for the ump-
teenth time. Jenna hadn't made her way in yet.
They'd agreed to meet here in the morning and
get some work done. She still had a few minutes but he couldn't help but be impatient. There
were things he needed to say to her. Questions
he needed to ask.

He hadn't played his cards right yesterday.
When Maxim had asked her if she needed Cabe
to come along with them, he should have inter-
jected right then and there. He should have said
something along the lines of *Of course I'm going
with her*. It just hadn't occurred to him that she
might actually decline his company on Maxim's
silly little tour.

He pinched the bridge of his nose and reclined

in the plush leather chair. He stared at the door again, willing it to open and for Jenna to walk in. He checked his phone again. No messages from her. It wasn't that she was late, just that she was usually early to every meeting.

He wanted to see her, first to make sure she was all right. And secondly to finally clear the air between them. They had to start behaving like adults about what had happened between them. They were attracted to each other and they'd acted on it. He wanted to reassure her that it wouldn't happen again. She didn't need to be so skittish around him. He couldn't wait to explain that to her. In fact, if she didn't come in within the next couple of minutes, he would walk back to their villa and go knock on her door.

But then she did walk in, and with one look at her face his resolve faded like a punctured balloon. Her eyes were red-rimmed and puffy, the tip of her nose crimson. Her cheeks held a light sheen. There was no question in his mind—Jenna Townsend had been crying, probably for most of the night.

240 MISS PRIM AND THE MAVERICK MILLIONAIRE

Maxim. That son of a bitch! But they'd left Maxim at the casino last night and walked back to their suite together. So what had happened?

He watched as she pulled out her laptop and took a seat across from him, a tight smile plastered on her face. "Good morning. Where would you like to start?"

Was she serious? Did she honestly think they were going to simply get to work like it was a typical morning?

She blinked when he didn't answer. "If we could get started, there's something I need to tell you as soon as we're finished."

Yeah, no kidding. He leaned toward her over the table. "Maybe you should just tell me now."

She shook her head. "No. It can wait. We should get some work done first."

Right. As if that was even a possibility in the state she was in. Not to mention his own. "Jenna. I insist."

She looked down, picked at her fingernail. Several beats passed in silence. As much as he wanted to, he couldn't push her. She clearly struggled to blurt out whatever her news was.

When she looked back up at him, the fake smile was back in place. "Please, Cabe. We need to get through these to-dos."

He nodded once. "We have plenty of time."

"That's just it—" She took a deep breath, but apparently couldn't make herself continue.

"What?" he prodded.

Her mouth opened. Then shut again. He waited for her to say something, anything. Nothing but more silence.

That was it. He'd had it. A man could only muster so much patience in the face of so much left unsaid. Cabe pushed out of his seat, slamming his pen on the table in frustration. The action startled her and she clamped a hand to her mouth.

"Jenna, I'm trying to understand what's happening here. Can you help me do that?"

To his horror, her eyes filled. What had he said to cause that?

"Are you crying?" he asked, his tone harsher than it probably should have been. He was just at such a loss about what to say or do. His arms ached to hold her, to tell her everything would be all right. But he had no doubt in his mind that any such gesture of comfort or physical closeness would be shunned.

Suddenly, she stood. "I'm leaving in a couple of hours, Cabe."

He couldn't have heard her right. Surely, whatever was upsetting her couldn't be that pressing. "You're leaving? Why in the world are you leaving? Our jet doesn't even return for another two days."

"I understand that," she told him. "I've booked a seat on a commercial flight."

"Why would you do that?"

"Because I'm dropping this project. I can no longer work on it. In fact, I can no longer work for *you*."

He couldn't have heard her right. Was she that regretful about their relationship? "Listen, Jenna. What happened between us will not happen again."

She shook her head, her cheeks growing a fiery red. "That's only part of it, Cabe."

"I get that I crossed a line."

Anguish flooded her eyes. "No. It's just— there's something you should know."

"I'm listening."

She sucked in a breath before answering. "You're going to get a call soon from your security personnel. Or maybe it will be Boston PD who notifies you first."

Cabe blinked. "Come again?"

Whatever he'd been expecting, it hadn't been anything along these lines. And then he remembered. "Does this have anything to do with the stolen bracelet?"

She nodded, swallowed hard. "I'm afraid so."

"Jenna, what's going on?"

Her face visibly crumbled and she held a hand to her midsection. In that instant, Cabe wanted nothing more than to hold her and find a way to alleviate her anguish. Clearly, Jenna thought she was at fault somehow for whatever had happened. Maybe she'd left the jewelry case unlocked and the thief had gotten to the jewelry that way. That certainly wouldn't be grounds for her dismissal. She had to know he didn't care. Everyone made mistakes. No bracelet, no matter how costly or valuable, was worth the pain she was clearly burdening herself with right now.

But he kept himself in check, stood firm where he was. It wouldn't do either of them any good to interrupt her. She had to continue. Had to get this over with. "See, there was a reason your security head suspected me."

He could have sworn the room spun around him. "What exactly are you saying? Did you have something to do with the theft after all? Just tell me, Jenna." Could she really have been that cunning? Kept it from him all this time?

He just needed her to come clean. He needed her to be straight with him.

"Cabe, I'm so sorry. I didn't know. It was my mother."

"Your mother? I don't understand. I thought they were investigating the security guard on duty that night?"

She pursed her lips, her eyes full of tears. "They are. He stole it with her help. Apparently, she'd been studying my routine. Knew where I kept my keys and told him everything. She gave him hints about what my passcode might be. She also told him to strike while I was away at that conference." She took another steadying breath. "He pretended to be interested in her in order to get her help."

His mouth had gone dry, which didn't matter. He couldn't seem to find any words anyway. Questions pummeled at him like a jackhammer in his brain.

"You have to believe I didn't know," she continued, her lip quivering. "I only just found out last night."

"Of course I believe you. I know you're not capable of being that duplicitous."

Jenna's shoulders visibly relaxed. "Thank you."

"I wish you'd just told me, instead of all the dramatics." He sighed, eyed the manila folder on his desk. All that would have to wait now. "I guess we should wrap up here. Then we can fly back together and deal with all this. I'll call the jet back today. We'll meet with Corporate Security as soon as we land."

Her eyes grew wide at his words. "Didn't you hear anything I said? My very own mother stole from you."

"I heard every word."

"She used me to do it."

"That's right. She used you. Am I missing something?"

"You said it yourself, Cabe. I didn't even know what she was up to."

"And none of that has anything to do with your competence. Or how valuable you are to this company." *To me*, he added silently.

"Nevertheless…" She looked away before adding, "There's no way I can continue to work for Jordan's Fine Jewelry as if none of this ever happened."

"You're not thinking this through, Jenna."

"I can't stay, Cabe." Her voice was low, pleading.

"What you really mean is that you *won't* stay," he corrected her. "The choice is yours to make. Yours alone."

She held up her hands. "That's what you're saying now. But this is just going to get uglier. You're going to end up regretting the day you hired me, that you had anything to do with Amanda Townsend's daughter."

He studied her, decided to call her bluff. "That's not what any of this is about."

"What does that mean?"

"It means that the real issue here is that you're blaming yourself. You're covering for Amanda. And as far as I can tell, you've been doing that your whole life."

She lifted her chin. "All that may be true. But it doesn't change anything."

"And that's the sad part. It doesn't change a thing. How long are you going to let Amanda's shortcomings impact your life?"

Suddenly, her eyes grew darker. She stepped closer to him, jabbed a finger in the air toward his chest. "You don't get to lecture me about this. You don't have any kind of cred when it comes to family dynamics."

The air crackled around them, the words hovering menacingly in the air. Jenna sucked in a breath, seemingly surprised by what she'd said.

He could only respond with silence. What was there to say? She wasn't wrong. He certainly couldn't confront her about the real reason he was so frustrated and angry about her decision. There was so much more at play here than Jenna's response to Amanda's crime.

The harsh reality was that she was running. From him. Here he was, offering to stand by her. To help her through this. And her response was to slam the door in his face, to totally shut him down.

It didn't even occur to her to turn to him, to trust him.

What did that say about him?

The silence prevailed until Jenna finally turned on her heel. "Goodbye, Cabe. I'll contact you in Boston via an attorney."

Well, that had gone well. Jenna adjusted her seat belt and tried to settle into the too-tight space. Just her luck, she had been seated between a heavyset gentleman and an overpacked older lady with a purse larger than she was. But when had luck ever been on her side?

The tears threatened to flow again and she fought them back. What good had crying ever done? She had to gather her wits about her and figure out what to do. First she needed an attorney. One who would no doubt take all her life savings. But she couldn't risk any less—her life depended on it.

Bad enough Amanda had devised the theft, but in true maddening form, she was now bragging about it. All over town. So much so that word had eventually gotten back to her brother, who was trying to convince Amanda to turn herself in. Before the authorities figured it all out and she had the book thrown at her. That was why Amanda had been trying to get hold of her so desperately. She wanted to get Jenna to try to convince her brother to back off.

The man next to her started to snore. A baby wailed from somewhere in the back. This was a far cry from the private jet she'd arrived on.

That was another lifetime ago. Back when she was still a professional with a career. She'd still had a future, maybe even a shot at happiness. Someone the likes of no other than Cabe Jordan had actually been attracted to. Jenna closed her eyes and tried to pretend that none of it had ever happened. That she was back to that first day on the jet with Cabe.

She remembered the look of shocked disappointment on his face when she'd told him about her leaving.

Snap out of it. She had to get that image out of her mind. She also had to forget about how he had looked at her that day near the waterfall. Like she was the only one who could have brought that smile to his face. Like she was the only woman for him.

There was no doubt that the next time he saw her, he would have nothing but disdain in his eyes. Jenna's stomach churned and it had nothing to do with the plane taking off. The things she'd said to him. Why couldn't she learn to control her mouth? He'd only been trying to help.

But she'd had to show him that he couldn't help her. There would be no white-knight scenario for Jenna Townsend. Cabe had his own demons. She wouldn't burden him with her own. He didn't know it now, but she was doing him a favor. Soon, he would realize it.

The sooner the better. For his sake.

Jenna surveyed the mess that was her mom's apartment. Take-out containers littered the floor, and empty beer bottles sat turned sideways on every flat surface. Various puddles of unknown liquids spotted the ground. And what in heaven's name was that smell?

She certainly wasn't in paradise any longer. In fact, Jenna would be hard-pressed to prove she hadn't imagined the whole Paraiso Resort and her time on it.

No, this was more like the depths of Hades. And she had her mother to thank for it.

She walked down the hall to the bedroom. Hard to believe, but there was an even bigger mess in here. An empty pizza box sat at her feet. Half-eaten bags of chips and candy cluttered most every surface. And of course, more assorted bottles lay strewn about the floor. She'd only been out of town a few days.

Looking for a priceless bracelet in this mess would be like looking for the proverbial needle in a haystack. Not that it was likely to be here. But she had to make sure.

Jenna felt the tears burn her eyes and a welt form in her throat. Why had she thought she could escape this? This was her life—this depressing, dirty town house and the woman who lived here, the burden of whose care fell solely on Jenna's shoulders. How could she have let herself forget that? How could she have let herself get close to anyone? Let alone someone like Cabe.

Her lips tingled as she remembered their kiss in the conference room. Such a mistake, she should have never let it happen. She thought she could let herself indulge, just one last time before he found out who Jenna Townsend really was. But then again, he'd always known. Everyone did.

Suddenly it was all too much. Her legs grew

weak and she perched herself on the edge of Amanda's bed. Several moments passed as she just sat there. Jenna felt nothing but shame. Even her anger had left her. All she held in her soul was a gnawing, hollow sense of shame.

"Hey, thought I might find you here." Her brother's voice startled her; she hadn't heard him come in.

She hurriedly wiped the moisture off her cheeks then turned and stepped over the garbage piles to give him a hug. "I just got here. Thought I'd look for the bracelet. Just in case."

Her brother let out a low whistle. "I doubt it's here, sis."

"It couldn't hurt to look, right?"

"Guess not."

But hours later, they were both ready to admit defeat. Despite having turned the mess in the apartment upside down, they couldn't find the bracelet anywhere. In fact, the place held nothing of value whatsoever. At least her mother's thievery had been a one-and-done affair.

Sam gave her shoulder a reassuring squeeze.

"We'll fix this, Jen. I swear I won't let you fall because of her latest stunt."

She managed a weak smile. "I'm not so sure this time's going to be fixable, Sam. Even if people believe I had no part in the theft, my reputation is ruined. What retail establishment is ever going to hire me again? I'm too much of a risk."

She choked as she said the last word. She was no longer employed with her dream company. She'd never be with Cabe again, not in any way. Reaching behind her, she found the edge of the bed once more. Her legs just weren't going to hold her up.

"Don't say that," Sam insisted. "We'll make them believe you. We'll make her." He pointed an accusatory finger at the empty bed, as if Amanda were still in it. "She'll explain what she did. Tell them that you had nothing to do with it."

"Who do you think is going to take her word for it?"

"Jen, we'll make them see the truth."

As usual, her mother had wreaked complete havoc in her children's lives.

"I have to go," she told her brother.

"Where are you going?"

"To find Amanda. I have to try to make at least part of this right." She turned on her heel and walked out the door before Sam could see the fresh round of tears.

Not that she really could make any of it right in any way. Not with the Jordans. And certainly not with Cabe. An anguished cry tore from her throat and she dropped down to sit on Amanda's cold stone stoop.

She thought about the way Cabe had smiled at her at the beach party as he'd sipped from the straw that she'd just used. The way his eyes had traveled over her that day in the boutique when she'd worn the designer gown. Now she wished she'd never gone to that party with him. She should have never set foot in that boutique.

Because it was all a fairy tale that she'd been living these past few days. One she now had to give up. It would have been so much easier on her heart never to have lived it at all.

CHAPTER NINE

SO SHE WANTED to see him.

Cabe set his office phone back down on the top of the mahogany desk, resisting the urge to listen to Jenna's message once more just to hear her voice. She'd left it at two o'clock in the morning. Apparently, neither of them had gotten much sleep last night. Hell, he hadn't gotten much sleep at all since he'd seen her last. He'd barely been able to think straight. Now she was requesting "time on his schedule" the same day he'd arrived back in Boston. That was exactly how she'd phrased it. So formal. So straightforward. As if nothing had ever happened between them. It would serve her right if he ignored her. Make her come to him.

He sighed. Of course he wouldn't do that. Instead, he typed out a text to her cell phone.

I have time right now. My office.

It took less than five minutes before he heard her knock on his door. He fixed his cuff links and stood. Maybe he'd finally get some answers. She opened the door and he motioned for her to come in. He lost his breath when she did.

So beautiful. The severe ponytail was back, as tight as he'd ever seen it. Her navy pin-striped suit—all business. Dark circles smudged her eyes. She looked utterly beat. And still, she was the most beautiful woman he'd ever laid eyes on. Insanity nearly took over his better judgment and he almost went to her. All he wanted to do right now was pull her into his arms, absorb her warmth, kiss those beckoning lips that so haunted his dreams. He wanted to tell her that everything would be all right, that he would see to it.

Instead, he tightened his fists at his sides.

She stopped in her tracks several feet away from him then took a deep breath. Definitely hesitant. Cabe perched himself on the edge of his desk, motioned to the chair opposite him. "Can

I get you anything?" he asked, just to get some kind of conversation going before sitting down.

She shook her head. "No, thank you. And I'd rather do this standing, if you don't mind."

Well, now he felt awkward as he'd already sat. But standing again would look silly. Wouldn't it? Damn it, she was the only woman in the world who could get him so riled. He made million-dollar decisions on a daily basis. But around her he didn't even know whether to sit or stand, for heaven's sake.

"It won't take long," she added.

He simply nodded for her to continue.

"I just wanted to return this." She stepped over and dropped something shiny and bright onto the desk in front of him.

The bracelet.

"How?"

"We found the thief, Sam and I. Convinced him to hand it over. The authorities are on their way to arrest him now." She pointed to the object that had caused so much havoc in their lives. "I assure you, it's the real piece."

Cabe could only stare. "I don't understand."

"It's simple. I made my mother tell me where your sneaky security guard could be found. Then Sam and I had a heart-to-heart with him."

He didn't like the sound of this, not at all. "Let me get this straight. You and your brother searched out and approached a known thug. Just to retrieve a stolen bracelet. Putting your very life at risk in the process."

She narrowed her eyes on him. "Hardly. We just convinced him it was only a matter of time before the cops came for him. He was almost relieved to dispose of it. Couldn't even fence the thing on the street. Too valuable. He didn't have those kinds of connections. Lord knows Amanda doesn't."

Cabe's heart pounded with anger. To think she had jeopardized her personal safety. For some bauble he honestly couldn't have cared less about.

"At least Jordan's has the piece back," Jenna said.

How could she be so flippant about this? "Look. You didn't need to risk your safety by

retrieving it. We had the matter under control."
That was a lie. Cabe hadn't even thought about
the cursed bracelet since the day Jenna had left
his office. He'd done absolutely nothing about its
theft. Not even so much as to call Jordan's Security and give them an update. That bracelet had
only caused one headache after another. But she
didn't need to know that. When he thought of the
danger she put herself in, he wanted to grab her
by the shoulders and shake her.

Then he wanted to kiss her until she finally
started to see some sense.

"I know it doesn't really solve anything," she
said, apologetically.

No, it didn't. Not at all. Which made it all the
worse. "What the hell are you trying to prove
here, Jenna?"

Ire flashed in her eyes. "I wasn't trying to prove
anything. Merely rectifying a mistake I made."

Cabe wanted to throw something. "There you
go again. *You* didn't make a mistake. You did
nothing wrong. *Amanda*, your mother, stole from

the store." He emphasized the name, hoping it would drive his point home.

No such luck. Her back stiffened before she spoke. "My mother was targeted by a charming con artist because of where I worked."

"Are you apologizing for where you chose to be employed?"

She actually stomped her foot. "I'm not apologizing at all. Not for getting the bracelet back. I'm merely returning it."

"Which you did by risking your own safety, going after a known thief. Can you not even see the danger you put yourself in?"

"I've been dealing with people like that thief since I can remember. My mother didn't exactly have high standards when it came to her boyfriends."

"How long are you going to let her run your life, Jenna? You quit your job because of her, you foolishly went and got the bracelet back to make up for her mistake. When are you going to realize that you have your own worth? Beyond the stain of your mother's reputation?"

She gasped. "I made my own decisions."

He actually laughed. "Do you really think that? You just keep trying to prove yourself."

Her jaw dropped. "Did you just accuse me of trying to prove myself to atone for who my mother is?"

"Don't you?"

She snorted a small laugh. "You have no idea how hypocritical that is."

The one word struck like a dart in his brain. "Hypocritical?"

"You really don't see it, do you? You've done nothing but reach for and achieve goal after goal, just to prove yourself worthy of the Jordan name. The whole world can see you're a credit to your parents. Everyone except you!" She threw her hands in the air. "It's almost as if... Oh, never mind!"

Cabe crossed his arms over his chest. "No, please. Continue. I'd really like to hear this."

"It's as if you have to ensure James and Tricia don't ever regret adopting you. Like you have to continually find ways to earn their love, only to come up short time and time again."

The room grew dark around him; he felt the muscles in his neck tighten to the point of pain. Jenna had no idea what she was talking about. Why in the world had he ever thought she might be someone who could understand? He'd been a fool to ever confide in her about his parentage.

"Thank you for bringing back the bracelet. Now, if you don't mind, I have a lot of work to do. On top of my regular workload, I no longer have any assistance with the Caribbean expansion."

Jenna flinched, his words finding their target. So be it. "That's it?" she asked incredulously.

"Yes. It is. I believe we've both said all there is to say to each other."

She shook her head and turned to the door, slamming it hard on her way out.

Cabe paced the length of the room and tried to get his pulse in check. It didn't help. All the confusion and frustration of the past two days formed into a barreling rage inside his chest. He turned with a vicious curse and landed a swift, hard kick to the parlor table in the center of his office. It landed with a thud so loud it must have resonated to the floor below. But he barely heard the noise over the roaring in his ears.

Cabe's administrative assistant knocked on his door again. This was probably the fourth or fifth time this morning. She'd been doing that, checking in on him, ever since the incident a few days back when he'd kicked the table over and caused such a loud ruckus. Apparently she wasn't buying Cabe's story that he'd tripped and toppled it accidentally. The interruptions were getting annoying. Not that he'd actually been focusing enough to get anything done. He hadn't been able to focus on anything since Jenna had left his office three days ago.

"Betty. I really am fine," he began. "You don't have to—" He stopped when he realized there was someone in the reception area behind her.

"Actually, Mr. Jordan. Your father is here to see you."

Cabe put down the spreadsheet he held in his hand. James was here? Now what? Then it occurred to him—his parents had no doubt heard about Jenna leaving their employ.

Cabe had some explaining to do.

Standing, he nodded at her. "Show him in."

James entered wearing jeans and a blue checked shirt, no tie. His father had a sharp head for business, but had never been interested in dressing the part.

"Father. I've been meaning to set up a time to talk to you. And Tricia."

"I figured I'd come by while you were in town. I probably should have called first."

Did he always have to sound so overly polite with him? "It's technically your company."

His father pulled out the chair opposite the desk and sat. "You run it. Although that's what I came to talk to you about. I hear we may be losing a valuable member of the Jordan team."

He should have seen this coming, Cabe thought. Very little happened within the business that James wasn't swiftly made aware of. He made it a point to know everything that went on with the company he started, regardless of who actually ran it.

"Jenna Townsend was on location to help me with the Caribbean expansion when things got a little…complicated."

"So I gathered. Was there more than one complication? In addition to the missing jewelry?"

At Cabe's puzzled expression, James continued. "Your reputation as a ladies' man somewhat precedes you, son. Jenna's a very attractive woman."

Cabe grunted. Despite ditching the photographer back at the island, it looked like the gossip mill still churned out its story.

"I'll squelch the rumors. This isn't a long-term concern."

James held up a hand. "That's not why I'm asking, not because of the business."

"It's not?"

James shook his head. "Your mom and I, we've known Jenna since she was a little girl. She hasn't had the easiest life."

Cabe barely suppressed a groan. "Don't I know it?"

His father's eyebrows lifted. "She confided in you?"

He hadn't really thought about it that way, but now that his father mentioned it… "I guess she did."

"That's surprising. She tends to keep that stuff about her family close to her chest."

"We had a few opportunities to talk." He looked his father square in the eye. "I sort of confided in her, too. I know we don't normally talk about it with anyone, but I told her the truth."

"The truth?"

"That I'm not really your son."

His father sucked in a breath. "Is that how you put it? When you told her?"

"More or less."

"That's how you see yourself, then. As not really my son."

How in the world had this conversation veered in this direction? They were supposed to be talking about Jenna and what it would mean to their business if she left the company.

"It's not like I don't realize how lucky I am. I owe everything to you and Tricia."

James nodded slowly. "You're not really my son and you owe us for bringing you up."

Well, when he phrased it that way... But, as off-putting as it sounded, it was essentially the truth.

"As parents, you did everything you could," Cabe reassured him.

"If that's the impression you have of us, we clearly needed to do more." He looked off to the side, summoning the words. "Listen, Cabe, your mother and I probably should have waited before adopting another baby. Tricia couldn't handle her grief, and I wasn't strong enough to help her. I was barely containing my own. But that doesn't mean you weren't wanted. Or loved."

James may as well have sucker punched him. A lump formed at the base of Cabe's throat. "Thank you for saying that."

"I should have said it years ago. And more." He swallowed visibly. "But I never found the right times. And frankly, I never found the courage. Until now. Better late than never, right?" James chuckled, thought it sounded false and the smile didn't reach his eyes.

"Truth be told," his father went on, "not only have you earned our respect repeatedly over the years, you've been a constant source of both joy and love in our lives, more so than we could have hoped that first day we brought you home. And I'm ashamed to admit that I didn't tell you that or show you nearly as often as I should have."

Or at all, Cabe thought. James's words were beyond unexpected. He'd never so much as uttered an affectionate word to him over the years.

The James Jordan sitting opposite him right now bore little resemblance to the distant and distracted man Cabe had grown up with.

Was Cabe mistaken or were his father's eyes actually shimmering with moisture? James was the strongest man he had ever known. Never once in his life had he seen him so much as shed a tear. He'd just appeared perpetually sad.

When James spoke again, his voice was thick. "You are and have always been my son."

Cabe had to remind himself to breathe.

The words hung powerfully in the air. Both men stared uncomfortably at each other for several moments. For the life of him, Cabe couldn't come up with a single thing to say.

Finally, James cleared his throat. "Now, where exactly do we stand with Jenna?"

Cabe blinked at the sudden question. His father was clearly ready to change the subject. Pushing his hair off his forehead, Cabe searched for a way to answer. How to describe where he stood with Jenna? "She's unlike anyone I've ever met. She's got an incomparable business sense, yet she's sensitive and so aware of the needs of others. She can be infuriatingly stubborn but somehow knows when to compromise. She can make me angry as a hornet one minute, and then make me laugh the next. I've never been with anyone like her."

"I see." James studied the carpet, didn't look up when he asked the next question. "Does she know?"

"Know what?"

His father looked at him as if he should be

wearing a dunce cap. Maybe he was right. But he was still trying to process the overwhelming conversation of a few minutes ago. "I mean, did you ever actually come out and tell her any of this?"

"Uh. No."

James shifted in his chair, uncomfortable again. "Listen, Cabe. Your mother and I haven't exactly been the most open or, God forgive me, the most willing, when it came to demonstrating affection. I've known that in my gut. But I guess what we just talked about drove it all home."

Another shocking admission. His father was making all sorts of confessions here.

"Maybe we're not the best examples to follow."

Cabe hadn't realized that he'd been following anyone's example. But he had to acknowledge James's point. In his last few conversations with Jenna, he'd been totally focused on her complete willingness to set aside her own needs for the sake of her family. He'd been trying to point out to her how wrong that was.

It was Cabe who was wrong; James had just shown him that. No, that wasn't correct. Jenna had been the one to show him. James had merely just confirmed her point.

Up until today, Cabe had been too blind to see what was so clear all along. He'd always had the love of his parents. They really did value and cherish him. They just had no idea how to show it.

At least Jenna had the courage to accept the family she had and to love them anyway. She was right to call him a hypocrite.

"What I'm trying to say is," James continued, "you've been a fighter your whole life. This is something worth fighting for. Jenna's not the type of woman you want to lose once you have her."

Clearly, James was no longer referring to the company.

CHAPTER TEN

JENNA TENSED WHEN her doorbell rang. She just couldn't bring herself to entertain the possibility that it might be the police. She had no clue what she would say to them if they were already here for her. Though it would have to count for something that the bracelet had been returned. Taking a fortifying breath, she yanked open her door. Then did a double take when she saw who her visitor was.

"Cabe? I thought you would have returned to Manhattan by now."

"Not yet. I had some agenda items to finish."

Her heart plummeted. He was here on some kind of business.

"I wanted to come by and tell you that you can relax. No one's going to press charges against your mother."

Could she have heard that right? "I don't understand."

"Roger, my head of security, is former Boston PD. He's still got a lot of connections. He'll make sure the authorities know you had nothing to do with the robbery. And he can put in a word on your mom's behalf, make sure she gets a break. They'll be easier to convince now that the item is back in its rightful place. And because she's seeking help for her addictions."

Jenna's relief almost had her knees buckling beneath her. That was an unexpected turn. She didn't want to look a gift horse in the mouth but the development begged a question. "But why would your security head do that?"

"Because I asked him to."

He had? Her mouth fell open. "I don't know what to say. Except that I can't thank you enough. Really, Cabe, that was above and beyond. You don't know how much I appreciate it."

But it still didn't explain why he was here, at her door. He could have called with the info. Or had his secretary do it even.

He surprised her further by asking, "Can I come in?"

Stepping aside, she motioned him inside and shut the door. His eyes grew wide when he saw her packed airline bag against the wall.

"Are you going somewhere?"

She nodded. "I have some interviews lined up. Out of state."

His lips thinned into a slim line. "I apologize. I should have called first."

Suddenly he was serious, matter-of-fact. His mouth didn't hold a hint of a smile. Still, all she could think about was how good it was to see him, just to have him in the same room. It didn't seem possible that fate had given her a chance to see him one more time. Taking a moment to study his face, she thought how haggard he looked now. Dark circles framed his weary bloodshot eyes. He clearly had not bothered to shave this morning.

"It's okay," she assured him. "I have some time." Though the truth was she'd actually be cutting it really close if she delayed any longer, barely giving herself enough time to get to the airport and check in. But she couldn't bear to send him away just yet. She missed him! She'd been walking around zombielike these past few days, barely able to function, the features of Cabe's face etched in her mind. The feel of his touch imprinted onto her skin. "Can I get you anything? Coffee?"

"Sure, that'd be great."

Jenna went to the still-warm coffeepot, half full. She was glad she hadn't had a chance to empty and rinse the carafe. When she returned, Cabe was sitting on her sofa, with her sketchbook lying open on the coffee table in front of him. He pointed to the page she'd been working on. "These are really good. Did you do them?"

She ducked her head at the compliment. "I try some designing in my spare time. Mostly necklaces."

He picked up the book and studied it. "I had no idea you designed jewelry."

Jenna set the coffee cup down, hoping he didn't notice the trembling in her hands. This conversation was so awkward. All she wanted to do was wrap her arms around his neck and feel his lips on hers. Instead, she was racking her brain trying to come up with what to say next.

"I don't know if it's any good," she replied with genuine doubt. No one had ever actually seen any of her sketches until now.

"You're full of surprises, Jenna."

Another awkward pause settled between them.

He inhaled a deep breath. "Jenna, you're unlike any woman I've ever met. You design jewelry. You have an amazing head for business. You charm everyone you meet. And you've done an amazing job of managing your severely troubled parent while raising yourself and a brother." He stood to face her, ran a finger down her cheek. A hot tingle ran up her spine at his touch, and the smell of his aftershave teased her senses. "You're one of the bravest people I know, man or woman."

Whoa. Jenna gave her head a shake. "Brave? How in the world am I brave in any way?"

"You really don't see it, do you? The way you put your mom first, despite what it's cost you.

That takes the kind of rare courage few people possess. You actually confronted a known criminal to rectify what she'd done." He visibly shuddered. "Please don't do anything like that ever again, by the way."

She sniffled on a laugh. "I won't—I promise."

He motioned toward her suitcase. "I know I have no right—but cancel those interviews. Say you'll stay, Jenna."

"You want me to stay at Jordan's Fine Jewelry?"

Cabe shook his head. "Not exactly."

She swallowed down the hope that had blossomed in her chest. How foolish of her. Of course she'd misunderstood him. Until she heard his next words.

"I want more than that. I want you to stay with *me*."

He grasped her hand in his. Jenna couldn't seem to make her brain work. Thoughts scrambled around in her head like fallen leaves during a windstorm. It was hard enough to wrap her mind around the fact that he was here, in her home. She couldn't process what he was telling her. It was simply too good to be true. "Cabe, what are you saying?"

"I'm saying that watching you walk out of my office that day nearly broke me. I haven't been able to sleep. I keep thinking about the way you felt in my arms, the way we were together on the island. I can't lose that, Jenna." He inhaled deeply. "I know I have a lot to work on. To make myself the kind of man you deserve. I just need you to be patient."

That settled it. She'd obviously awoken to some alternate reality. The world had turned upside down. Cabe Jordan was pleading with her to be patient with him. Asking her to understand that he would work hard to become the right man for her.

"I know it's a lot to ask," Cabe continued. "You've obviously had the patience of a saint over the years. You've raised yourself and your brother on your own, made sure your mother didn't completely self-destruct. It's unfair to ask you to extend yourself any more for my sake."

Tears sprang into her eyes. She reached for him, clasped his unshaven chin in her hand. "As far as courage goes, you have it in spades, Cabe Jordan."

It was his turn to look shocked. So she explained, "You've done your utter best all your life to try and make your parents happy. Even knowing that it may never be enough. That's the definition of loyalty. Of bravery. You're everything anyone could ever hope for in a son."

He turned his face in her cupped palm, exactly as he had that day at the waterfall. "Then why? Why did you feel the need to leave at first?"

She choked down on a sob. "How can you ask that? I could barely face you. By then you meant so much to me. How was I supposed to ask you to accept the fact that my own mother had stolen from you?"

"You beautiful, silly fool. You have no idea how you impressed me."

She was definitely hearing things. "Impressed you?"

He nodded. "You could have surrendered Amanda to the authorities. Then gone back to your job and lived your life. No one would have blamed you for doing so. Instead, you quit the job you loved and hired an attorney for her. You might not realize what kind of a person that makes you, but I do."

"Is that really how you see me?"

"It's exactly how I see you. I just didn't know how to tell you any of that."

Just those simple words, and somehow the steel bands around her heart snapped open. Cabe didn't judge her on who her mother was or where she came from. He saw her strengths and judged her on her actions. He saw Jenna for who she was.

Maybe he could help her see it, too.

He pulled her to him then, kissing her deeply and holding her tight against his frame. "Besides, by then I'd already fallen in love with you. You could have asked me anything."

Her heart had not only just sprung free but Jenna was certain it would burst any moment now. "You love me?" she stammered, her mind on the verge of going numb.

He didn't need to use any words when he answered her.

* * *

"You look beautiful, Jenna."

Jenna turned away from the boutique mirror to face the two ladies helping her get ready. "Do you really think so, Seema?"

Seema beamed back at her. "Yes. That dress may as well have been made for you." She walked over to give Jenna a tight squeeze around the shoulders. Martine, the saleswoman who had encouraged her to fatefully try on this very dress all those weeks ago, gave her a conspiratorial wink.

A low rumble of thunder sounded through the walls from outside. The forecast this morning called for a major storm far off the coast. No doubt she and Cabe would be saying their vows under a cloudy sky with sprinkles of rain. None of it mattered or could make so much as a dent in her joy. She could weather any storm with Cabe by her side.

As she turned back to her reflection in the mirror, Jenna's heart did a little jump at the sight. Was that really her staring back from the glass?

Jenna had known the moment Cabe asked her to marry him that this would be her bridal gown.

She also knew there was no other place on earth she'd rather have her wedding than here, at the Paraiso Resort.

And no other man she wanted to spend the rest of her life with.

Cabe was in the process of admiring his bride and marveling at his luck when his father surprised him by standing up. His parents were seated at the closest table to the wedding dais, along with Seema and Jenna's brother. Jenna's mom remained in Boston, getting the rehabilitation treatment she so desperately needed. That had been part of the deal when the Jordans agreed not to press charges.

His father picked up his wineglass and raised it, clearing his throat to get everyone's attention. A toast. The roar of chatter gradually diminished as their guests noticed.

Cabe inhaled and braced himself. He honestly had no idea what his father might say; it hadn't even occurred to him to ask his father to speak. No doubt his speech would be all about the growth of Jordan Enterprises under Cabe's leadership. Or something.

He was wrong. In fact, his dad surprised him and didn't even mention business.

James took a deep breath and began. "I'm not sure if I can find the word to adequately express what I want to say. But here goes," James said and smiled in a way that didn't quite reach his eyes. He turned toward the wedding guests. "My son has managed to do so much in his life. He's been a terrific son and he's achieved more into his thirties than most men do in a lifetime. And now he's managed to snare himself a wife as accomplished and beautiful as Jenna."

Cabe heard Jenna gasp in surprise as she reached for his hand and gave it a gentle squeeze. He in turn clung to her fingers.

His father went on. "You've done so much for yourself, Cabe. All on your own. We should have been there for you more than we were. For that,

I can only ask your forgiveness." James looked him straight in the eye as he said the last word.

Cabe could only stare frozen, unable to come up with anything appropriate to say or do. He stole a glance at his mother and immediately realized there'd be no help from that corner—she was definitely crying. An awkward silence ensued.

James took a deep breath, opened his mouth to presumably say more, but then suddenly shut it again. He looked to the ground, clearly struggling to find the wherewithal to continue.

Jenna's hand slowly released his. He felt the loss of her touch immediately. But then she did something so simple yet so powerful, it reaffirmed why he'd fallen head over heels in love with her in the first place. She stood and slowly started to clap. It wasn't long before the rest of their guests joined her. The look of gratitude and relief on his father's face said it all. No, not his father, Cabe corrected himself. His dad. James held the expression of a man who'd just been rescued from drowning.

And they had Cabe's new bride to thank for it.

* * *

Once the applause died down and everyone had lowered their glasses, Jenna looked up to find Cabe holding out his hand to her.

She stood and he took her by the waist, led her to the dance floor. As they swayed to the rhythmic reggae song, he leaned over to whisper in her ear. "I love you, Mrs. Jordan."

The words, coupled with the magic of the moment, brought tears of happiness to her eyes. "And I've always loved you, Mr. Jordan."

He laughed and it sent pure pleasure through her whole body, down to her toes. "If only I'd known. Think of all the time we've wasted."

"It was your fault for never asking me to prom."

He affectionately nipped at her ear. "Perhaps. But you know, *you* could have asked me."

"Hmm. You're right. We'll just have to find a way to make up for lost time," she teased.

He brushed his lips against hers. "I can't wait to start."

Jenna knew they already had.

* * * * *

MILLS & BOON®
Large Print – August 2017

The Italian's One-Night Baby
Lynne Graham

The Desert King's Captive Bride
Annie West

Once a Moretti Wife
Michelle Smart

The Boss's Nine-Month Negotiation
Maya Blake

The Secret Heir of Alazar
Kate Hewitt

Crowned for the Drakon Legacy
Tara Pammi

His Mistress with Two Secrets
Dani Collins

Stranded with the Secret Billionaire
Marion Lennox

Reunited by a Baby Bombshell
Barbara Hannay

The Spanish Tycoon's Takeover
Michelle Douglas

Miss Prim and the Maverick Millionaire
Nina Singh

MILLS & BOON®
Large Print – September 2017

The Sheikh's Bought Wife
Sharon Kendrick

The Innocent's Shameful Secret
Sara Craven

The Magnate's Tempestuous Marriage
Miranda Lee

The Forced Bride of Alazar
Kate Hewitt

Bound by the Sultan's Baby
Carol Marinelli

Blackmailed Down the Aisle
Louise Fuller

Di Marcello's Secret Son
Rachael Thomas

Conveniently Wed to the Greek
Kandy Shepherd

His Shy Cinderella
Kate Hardy

Falling for the Rebel Princess
Ellie Darkins

Claimed by the Wealthy Magnate
Nina Milne

0817 Rom LP